WI MISS

Long behi him di to burst of flame encircle the muzzle of Thyman's revolver. A bullet sizzled past close to Longarm's ear.

Longarm's Colt roared, the backstrap pushing hard into the web of his hand. The bullet struck Thyman about four inches above his belt buckle, doubling him over at the waist even more effectively than Longarm's punch had done the afternoon before.

Not one to take unnecessary chances with someone who wanted to kill him, Longarm took careful aim and fired twice more.

Thyman dropped onto the sidewalk. He would not be moving again, not under his own power, anyway.

DON'T MISS THESE
ALL-ACTION WESTERN SERIES
FROM THE BERKLEY PUBLISHING GROUP

THE GUNSMITH by J. R. Roberts
Clint Adams was a legend among lawmen, outlaws, and ladies. They called him . . . the Gunsmith.

LONGARM by Tabor Evans
The popular long-running series about Deputy U.S. Marshal Long—his life, his loves, his fight for justice.

SLOCUM by Jake Logan
Today's longest-running action Western. John Slocum rides a deadly trail of hot blood and cold steel.

BUSHWHACKERS by B. J. Lanagan
An action-packed series by the creators of Longarm! The rousing adventures of the most brutal gang of cutthroats ever assembled—Quantrill's Raiders.

DIAMONDBACK by Guy Brewer
Dex Yancey is Diamondback, a Southern gentleman turned con man when his brother cheats him out of the family fortune. Ladies love him. Gamblers hate him. But nobody pulls one over on Dex . . .

WILDGUN by Jack Hanson
The blazing adventures of mountain man Will Barlow—from the creators of Longarm!

TEXAS TRACKER by Tom Calhoun
Meet J. T. Law: the most relentless—and dangerous—manhunter in all Texas. Where sheriffs and posses fail, he's the best man to bring in the most vicious outlaws—for a price.

TABOR EVANS

JOVE BOOKS, NEW YORK

LONGARM AND THE POISONERS

A Jove Book / published by arrangement with the author

PRINTING HISTORY
Jove edition / April 2003

For information address: The Berkley Publishing Group, a division of Penguin Putnam Inc.,
375 Hudson Street, New York, New York 10014.

ISBN: 0-515-13513-5

A JOVE BOOK®
Jove Books are published by The Berkley Publishing Group, a division of Penguin Putnam Inc.,
375 Hudson Street, New York, New York 10014.
JOVE and the "J" design
are trademarks belonging to Penguin Putnam Inc.

PRINTED IN THE UNITED STATES OF AMERICA

10 9 8 7 6 5 4 3 2 1

Chapter 1

Longarm was whistling as he trotted up the steps to the main entrance of the gray stone Federal Building. If he had been ten years old, it might reasonably have been said that he skipped up the stairs. But mature men do not skip. Deputy United States marshals in particular are not known for frivolities like skipping. Therefore, Deputy Marshal Custis Long did not skip. He trotted. Albeit with a light and cheerful gait that disclosed to all the world his good humor on this gloriously beautiful spring morning.

He paused at the top of the steps to take a final drag on the short end of an excellent cheroot, and flipped the butt aside. Down at street level, a trio of high school girls looked at him and tittered, one of them blushing red as a Hudson's Bay trade blanket at whatever the other two said to her.

Longarm kept himself from bursting into laughter. But only because the girls would have thought he was laughing at them had he done so. In fact, in their youthful innocence, they contributed to his already excellent state of mind. They were cute. And he was happy. That was all there was to it.

He could not help but acknowledge, though, that those

youngsters seemed to find him attractive, and for that he was pleased. Not that he had any interest in schoolchildren. But their admiration pleased him. All the more so if their interest might translate to a similar reaction by Miss Edith Kessler, who he had met last night at what he had feared would be a staid and stuffy affair. Instead, thanks to the presence of Miss Kessler, it had been a delight, a joy, a revelation. Longarm sighed.

He stood for another moment or two drinking in the soft, cool morning air. And wondering what Miss Kessler's opinion had been.

Longarm was almost totally lacking in matters of personal vanity. But he was certainly aware that more than one handsome young woman had been known to find him attractive even though his appearance was not the conventional ideal.

He was taller than average, standing some inches above six feet in height, and he had a lean, robust build with wide shoulders, a flat belly, and a horseman's powerful legs. He had dark brown hair and a sweeping brown mustache, liquid brown eyes that could soften a maiden's resistance or chill an enemy's gut, and a tanned and craggy face that he himself always thought rather ordinary.

He customarily wore brown corduroy trousers, checked shirt and calfskin vest, and a brown tweed coat, the whole set off from bottom to top by black stovepipe cavalry boots and a flat-crowned brown Stetson hat. In between he carried the tools of his trade: a black gunbelt rigged for a cross-draw of his .44-caliber Colt double-action revolver, and out of sight in a vest pocket, a custom-made, brass-framed .44-caliber derringer pistol. The badge that attested to his authority was normally out of sight, pinned inside a wallet in an inside coat pocket.

Longarm took a few deep breaths, enjoying the sights and sounds of the morning traffic on Denver's Colfax Avenue, then turned and opened the door leading to the mundane realities of the workaday world.

"*Good* morning, Henry," he called to the marshal's mousy and bespectacled little office clerk, an appearance that was a total lie as Henry had cojones as big as any deputy on the staff, and had been pressed into active service more than once in the past.

"Good Lord, Long," Henry blurted out. "You're on time."

"On a beautiful day like this? I should think so. It's good to be up and about, you know."

"Longarm! It is gray, drizzling, dreary as it can be out there. What put you in such a . . . no, never mind. You might tell me, and I really don't want to know her name or any of the particulars."

"What makes you assume it's a woman?" Longarm removed his hat and sailed it across the room, scoring a perfect ringer atop the hat rack that stood in the corner there. There were days when he tried that and missed. But not today. Today was really quite perfect.

"Custis, with you it's always a woman. Nothing else puts that kind of spring in your step."

"You judge me harshly," Longarm said accusingly.

"I judge you realistically," Henry countered. "But I know what's going to bring you back down to earth."

"Mm?"

Henry turned his head and pointed with his chin toward the closed door leading into the private office of their boss, William Vail, United States Marshal for the first District Court of Colorado, U.S. Justice Department. "Billy is not in your kind of good mood this morning, Custis."

"Something wrong?"

"He'll tell you about it."

Longarm headed toward one of the chairs so he could wait until Billy Vail was ready for him, but Henry said,

"Don't bother with that. He said you should come in as soon as you arrive. I just hope the shock of seeing you here on time won't be enough to do him in."

Longarm tapped softly on the door before opening it, then let himself in to the inner sanctum. "You wanted me, Boss?"

Billy Vail had a round face, rosy complexion, and a head that was almost completely innocent of any hair. He looked something like a cherub. But then Billy Vail's appearance was surely one of God's little jokes. No clueless political appointee, Billy had been a Texas Ranger in his younger years. He had put his fair share of desperados six feet underground; his share and then some. Longarm did not just like Billy, he respected the marshal too.

Vail appeared startled. He pulled a watch from his vest and checked the time. Stood and walked to the door to peer into the outer office and check his time against that of the big Regulator wall clock there, then looked at his watch again. Without comment, none being necessary, he returned to his desk and motioned Longarm to a chair.

"You know how I hate political hacks," he said. It was not posed as a question.

"Yes, I do."

"Last night I received a visit from two of them." The marshal slapped a sheet of paper that lay on his desk. His expression suggested he would prefer to crumple it up and throw it away. "The governor's hey-boy came to call."

"Alkyser?"

"That is the greasy little bastard, yes. I tell you, Custis, just looking at that man makes me want to run take a bath."

"He isn't my favorite person either."

"I suppose everyone who thinks of himself as a great man ought to have some kiss-ass toadies to fawn over him and tell him how wonderful he is, and I wouldn't think it would be easy to find candidates for the position.

No decent or reasonable man would want to do it. I suppose it takes phonies like Alkyser to make phonies like our governor happy. But I do wish the saints would preserve the rest of us from them."

"Yes, sir." Billy really was upset to be going on this openly about it, Longarm knew. "Good thing neither of us works for the state, isn't it, Boss?"

Vail glowered. "Fortunately for us, that is true. Unfortunately for us, we sometimes . . . too damned often . . . get caught in their web of stupidity."

"The U.S. Attorney has been requested to provide cooperation, is that it?" Longarm guessed.

"In a nutshell, yes."

"And it's something you really don't want to do." It took no special genius to add that bit to his guesswork.

"Again, yes." Billy thumped the desk with his fist. "Dammit, Long, you know how busy we are."

"Yes, I do."

"We're short two deputies as it is, and Dutch is on assignment transporting prisoners down in New Mexico, and Jerome Hanratty has a bad case of diarrhea and can't travel right now."

What Jerome actually had—which Longarm knew and Billy Vail did not—was a new mistress that he couldn't bear to be apart from more than a couple hours at a time. Far from being afflicted with the runs, Deputy Hanratty was quite thoroughly full of shit. But Longarm did not consider it his place to be the one to say so. When his dick wasn't doing all his thinking, Hanratty was a pretty good deputy. And everybody makes a mistake now and then. Why, even Longarm thought he made a mistake once. He was wrong about that, of course.

"Now we get this." Billy whacked the sheet of paper again.

"And that would be . . . ?"

"We are being asked to investigate a death, Long."

"All right."

"A death by natural causes."

"Pardon me, Boss? Did you say . . . ?"

"I did. Natural causes," Billy repeated. "Natural damned causes."

"And this requires investigation by a deputy United States marshal," Longarm said, expressionless.

"In this instance, apparently it does." The marshal shook his head. "Stupid as that is, it is true, Custis."

Longarm pulled out a cheroot, offered one to Billy, who declined, and lit the smoke, forgetting that Billy was on an anti-tobacco kick at the moment. Apparently the boss forgot about that too, because he did not object to Longarm's aromatic smoke filling the office.

"Do you know Hart County?"

"Colorado?"

Vail nodded.

"Over on the west slope, right?"

"That is the place, yes. County seat is Weirville. Population . . . I don't know . . . not very damn many, I shouldn't think. And somewhat fewer now than there used to be. That is to say, several people have died there in recent months."

"Of natural causes," Longarm said.

"Exactly. Never mind that people die of natural causes all over the damned place every day of the year. Including in Weirville."

"So what makes this different?"

"Apparently there is a county commissioner over there who is convinced there is some sinister reason why people die in his county."

"Has he considered filing suit against God?" Longarm asked.

"Don't suggest that. The imbecile might do it, and the judiciary would not appreciate your help if he does."

"Yes, sir."

"Before you ask, there is absolutely no reason I can think of to take this on under federal jurisdiction. Particularly so since no crime seems to have been committed. Certainly none that anyone knows about. But we are permitted . . . in this case obligated . . . to provide assistance to local government upon request."

"And we have such a request here, is that it?"

"Oh, do we ever. This county commissioner who insists on fabricating conspiracies out of whole cloth controls a rather influential voting bloc in the western reaches of the state. He holds considerable sway in the state legislature, and when he makes a personal appeal to the governor . . . who is up to something, God knows what, and needs the support of those legislators . . . well, his pleas will be heard."

"So the county hack lets the guv know that he'd best jump when the whip is cracked, then the gubner calls upon our intrepid U.S. Attorney with the sort of request that isn't about to be denied, and that worthy gentleman dumps the problem on the broad shoulders of his U.S. marshal, who in turn calls in an innocent deputy, who is expected to take a firm grip on the shitty end of the stick. Is that about it, Boss?"

"Except for the depiction of said deputy as being innocent . . . yes." Billy smiled for the first time since Longarm entered his office. "Welcome to the real world, Custis. You can have this." Billy picked up the offending paper and extended it to Longarm. "It will tell you everything I know about the request. See Henry for your travel vouchers. And Custis."

"Yes, Boss?"

"For God's sake don't waste any time with this crap, will you? Just go over there and show the colors. Let the idiot know we and the U.S. Attorney and the governor and all the members of the choir take his needs very, very seriously. Then brush the silly son of a bitch off and get back here so you can get some real work done for me. Fast. All right?"

"Quick and easy," Longarm promised with a smile.

He did not intend to lie to Billy. He really didn't.

Chapter 2

It isn't all that difficult to get from Denver to Weirville, Colorado. Usually. Take a train west through Central City and Fairplay to Buena Vista, then a coach across Monarch Pass, change express lines at Montrose, and then it's an easy run on to Hart County.

Or take a train south to Walsenburg, and a coach through LeVeta Pass to Alamosa, change there for the stage through Wolf Creek Pass to Durango and then to Cortez, change lines again, and run up to Hart County.

Easy enough. At certain times of year. Spring was not one of those times of year.

"You do whatever pleases you, Custis," Henry told him, "but the last report I got was that the passes to the west are still blocked. It could be weeks before anybody can get a coach through, and even then it's not the sort of thing you'd want to count on." Without a trace of a smile he added, "Or you could cross by way of Norwegian snowshoes and find a coach on the other side."

Longarm ignored that and asked, "What d'you suggest as an alternative?"

"If it was me . . . and mind you I'm glad that it isn't . . . I think I'd take the rails north to Cheyenne, then turn west to Rawlins. You can get a coach there south to Baggs. I don't know if they run any further than that. You might have to hire a horse to take you the rest of the way. Depending. At least you won't have to worry about being snowed in for days or weeks."

"I was hoping to make a quicker trip than that," Longarm grumbled.

Henry shrugged. "Go ahead and try the direct route if you like. But if you do, I'd still recommend you avoid Wolf Creek Pass. That one's a son of a bitch when it starts to melt free. Mud slides during the day with trees and rocks coming down the mountain at you, then everything freezes over again at night so the horses can't travel without falling and breaking their legs. I'd rather go Wolf Creek when it's snow-packed than melting. And who knows, maybe Monarch will be open by the time you get there."

"But you don't think so," Longarm said.

"But I don't think so," Henry agreed.

Longarm sighed. "I'll go the Wyoming route. But give me plenty of vouchers, will you? And don't be getting on my back if I decide to buy a horse instead of hiring one. I don't want to lock myself in to coming back the same way just to return the damn horse. If I buy one, we can just turn it over to the Army Remount Service here at home and get them to reimburse the office for it."

"Fair enough. I'll take care of it."

"You are a good man, Henry."

"Not everybody knows that, Custis. I'm glad you are one of my admirers." Henry laughed when he said it, and Longarm wondered if the unassuming little fellow knew that Deputy Marshal Long indeed was an admirer of his.

Henry collected a thick sheaf of the government forms that would enable Longarm to hire services and sign for them without having to worry about carrying cash except for his personal needs. He gave them to Longarm with his standard wishes that the deputy have good luck. And stay safe.

Rawlins was mighty well named, Longarm thought, if they would just remove that "lins" part and call it plain old Raw. Which it was. Begun as a railroad camp, it served now as a commercial and transportation hub—stagecoach and freight distribution alike—for a part of Wyoming that was probably bigger than some entire states back East.

Raw it was and busy, blustery, and full of, well, mud. The damned streets were pure mud now that the frost was coming out of the ground. Longarm collected his gear from the train's baggage car, and made a face when he stepped off the railroad depot platform into the cold mud of Rawlins.

He hated getting the thick, sticky stuff on his boots—back in Denver he'd only a couple days ago had them newly blacked and waxed, and now look at them—and now found himself standing so deep in the mud that it flowed completely over the foot part of the boots. He could actually feel the cold seeping through the leather. He shuddered.

Still, he hadn't come here to play the dandy. He had a job of work to do. He headed directly from the Union Pacific depot to the nearest stagecoach express company.

"D'you travel to Baggs?"

"Aye, we do."

"I'd like passage on the next available coach then, please."

"That would be daybreak day after tomorra," the clerk told him.

"Damn. There's no way I can leave sooner?"

"O' course you can. Just start walkin' south. Our coach will catch up an' let you aboard sometime around noon the day after tomorra."

"Thank you."

"You're welcome. Do I take it you'll be wanting a seat on that coach then?"

"I would, sir."

"If you'd care t' pay for your ticket now, mister, you'll have your spot reserved."

Longarm brought out his wallet, but instead of laying down money, he opened it to show his badge. "I assume you have a contract to carry mail?" One of the requirements for a common carrier with a mail-delivery contract was that federal peace officers and certain postal employees were entitled to ride along with the mail free of charge. Longarm needed no ticket.

The clerk sighed. Then smiled again. It wasn't his money or his coach line, after all. "I'll see to it that you have your seat." He leaned close and examined the badge before he added, "Deputy Marshal."

"Thanks. Could I trouble you for a recommendation about where I can put up for the night?"

"Around the corner and one block down, then turn left. There's a boardinghouse where we contract for our drivers an' messengers to stay. They tell me it's decent. Not fancy, though."

"I don't need fancy, but I do appreciate decent."

"Biggest house on the block. Painted blue."

"Painted? I'll be damned."

"Aye. Fella that owns it is peculiar that way. Paints his place a different color the fall of every year. Come the next fall, the wind an' blowin' sand has scrubbed the paint all away so's you can't hardly tell what the year's color was. Dunno why he does it, but I expect it must please him and his missus, an' when you come right down to it, that's reason enough."

"Thank you, sir. I'll go look for a blue house and tell them you sent me."

"Then I'll be seein' you along about the break o' day, day after tomorra."

"That you will, sir." Longarm touched the brim of his Stetson, bent, and picked up his gear again.

He had no trouble at all identifying the boardinghouse. Every other building he saw in Rawlins was bare, sand-blasted wood turned gray from the sun and badly warping in the dry air of this high desert country.

The room was as the stage-line clerk had said, decent although not fancy. Longarm paid for it with one of the vouchers Henry gave him, and left his things there while he went out in search of a meal, then perhaps afterward a drink and an evening's entertainment since he was going to have to be here for a spell.

Chapter 3

Longarm walked out of the café, his belly full and contentment adding its warmth to his sense of well-being. The meal had been good, the early evening air was soft and pleasant, and his mood was excellent. He paused on the board walkway to light a cheroot, then flipped the spent match into the mud of the street when he was done.

The man who ran the café said there was a saloon in the next block over that catered to the locals. A man could find a quiet drink and a friendly card game there, the café owner claimed. Longarm intended to verify that reputation with his own experience.

He turned toward the place in question, only to be stopped short by a sound of loud thumping and squealing behind him.

Worried that someone must surely be in trouble, Longarm spun around and dashed to the street corner. A couple dozen feet away a man was having trouble with his horse.

The horse had fallen at least once, for its near flank was plastered thick with mud. The man held a club in one hand and a lead rope in the other. He seemed intent on beating the horse down to the ground again.

As Longarm stood watching, the man yanked hard on

the rope, dragging the terrified horse to its knees. He swung the club in a sweeping blow just as the horse tried to struggle onto its feet again. The club missed the horse's head, which had been the original target, but smashed with a dull, moist thump on the side of the animal's neck.

The horse squealed and tried to back away, its hoofs sending globs of cold mud high into the air. Some of the mud wound up on the owner's face, further enraging the already furious man, who began screaming curses at the horse.

Longarm scowled. A man might have the right to discipline his own animal, but dammit, that did not give him license to use language like that when there likely were ladies and small children within hearing.

The tall deputy jammed the cigar between his teeth and stepped down into the mud of the street, approaching the man from behind.

The fellow yanked on the lead rope again, and prepared to take another swing at the horse's head. When he pulled the club back ready for another swing, Longarm reached out and took hold of his wrist. The attempted blow came up short.

The man whirled about, both surprise and redoubled fury etched on features that had turned a deep scarlet.

The fellow might have been a nice-enough-looking man in normal times. He was as tall as Longarm and heavier-built. He wore rough clothing, and was badly in need of a shave and a haircut, but had clean-cut features and all his teeth. He did, however, seem to have something of a problem controlling his temper.

"Why, you fancy-dressed son of a bitch, don't you know no better'n to interfere? Get the fuck outa here."

Longarm gave him a tight smile that held not the least hint of humor in it. "Friend, your language is a mite rough for town streets. There's ladies inside there." He nodded his head toward the nearest building. He had no idea if there were women present or not. But then he doubted that this man knew either, and the possibility certainly existed.

"Fuck them an' you too, asshole." The man tried to jerk his hand away from Longarm's grasp.

Longarm still had hold of the fellow's wrist. He dug his fingers into the gap between the thin arm bones just above the wrist, pressing hard on the tendons that lay there. The man cried out and lost his grip on the club.

"You son of a bitch!" he shrieked.

"I told you once already, mister. Stop your cussing in public."

"I'll do anything I damn please, you bastard."

"Then you'll do it in the privacy of a jail cell," Longarm told him in a mild tone of voice.

The man either did not hear, or chose not to heed Longarm's well-intentioned warning. He began cussing again all the louder and all the more vituperously, ending with something about "gonna show you, fucker" as he bent down to retrieve the fallen club from the muddy street.

His horse chose that moment to seek its freedom, rearing onto his hind legs and turning to run.

The man still held his grip on the lead rope, which he seemed to have temporarily forgotten. He had not, however, loosened that grip. A thousand pounds of muscle pulled at his arm while the fellow was unprepared, and the natural result of an application of superior weight and leverage was what one might expect. The man was pulled over backward and sprawled full-length in the mud of the Rawlins street.

"God *damn* it!" he roared as the horse broke away and bolted across to the other side of the street.

The man came sputtering and fuming to his feet, his clothing and half his face layered thick with the sticky mud. "You son of a *bitch*!" He fumbled at his waist for a holster that had gotten turned around so that his revolver was now at his back. He found the problem, and turned the belt so he could drag the gun out.

Longarm had no idea who or what the idiot intended to shoot, but quite apart from the fact that he did not want to be shot himself, he did not want this fellow to be spraying bullets down the streets of Rawlins in any direction.

Longarm stepped forward and took hold of the revolver. He twisted, and the gun came free in his hand as its owner cried out in pain from the trigger guard cutting into his flesh.

"Damn you to hell, you cocksucking son of a bitch."

"You do have a problem with that foul mouth o' yours, don't you," Longarm observed.

"I'm gonna kill you, you bastard."

Longarm only smiled at him. But then, why not? The gent—who in truth was no gentleman—had just gone and threatened violence upon the person of a deputy U.S. marshal. And that was a federal offense punishable by . . . well, by whatever the hell; Longarm couldn't recall that right at the moment. Point was, it was a federal offense and cause for prosecution.

The man balled his hands into fists, reared back, and let fly with a roundhouse right.

Which proved to be something of a mistake.

Longarm swayed back from the waist to let that punch go by.

Then he took a step forward and went about the task of demonstrating to this hot-tempered idiot just how serious an error he'd committed.

Chapter 4

Longarm's first blow was a solid right hand that started at waist level and swept up and forward until it landed, knuckles extended, wrist-deep in the fellow's breadbasket.

The breath was driven out of him and he bent at the waist. Longarm swiveled a quarter turn to his left, raised a clubbed fist, and smashed it down just as hard and nasty as he could on the man's unprotected right temple. The fellow dropped facedown in the mud and lay there as still as a corpse. Which for one awful moment Longarm thought he just might be.

Longarm took hold of his collar and lifted his face and upper body out of the mud. He used the toe of his boot to nudge the unconscious man onto his back, then bent and cleared some of the caked mud out of the gent's nostrils so he could breathe properly. Longarm couldn't find a clean spot on the fellow's shirt on which to wipe the mud off his hand after that, so he settled for picking up the man's hat and scraping his fingers clean on it . . . on the inside of the hat actually, as that was the cleanest part he could find.

"You there, son," he said to one of the dozen or so spectators who had gathered. "Want to earn a dime?"

"Yes, *sir*!" the kid piped up quickly. The boy looked to be ten or eleven years old, all ears and eyes and freckles.

"I'd like you to go find your town marshal or one of his deputies and fetch them here."

"No need for that, mister," a voice said from behind Longarm. "I'm here already."

Longarm turned to see a middle-aged man with a potbelly, a mustache almost as fierce as Longarm's own, and a polished steel badge on the lapel of his suit coat.

"I'm town marshal here. Want to tell me why you've assaulted one of my favorite citizens?"

"Hey!" the boy yelped. "What about the dime you promised me?"

Longarm smiled and said, "Well, now, you didn't actually do any work. But how's about I give you a nickel as a retainer fee. And if I need any other errands run, I'll look for you first. Is that fair?"

"Yes, sir." The kid grinned. "But I'd ruther have the dime."

"And so you shall. If there's a next time."

"Okay."

Longarm fished the change from his pocket and looked at it. He had no nickel. But he did have a dime. He laughed and gave that to the boy. Then he turned back to the local lawman. "This man is my prisoner," he said, pointing down at the no-longer-belligerent man on the ground. That one was just beginning to come around, and was struggling to get his wits and balance back to the point where he could sit up.

"Prisoner?"

Longarm introduced himself.

"I'm Dave Childers, deputy. Pleased to meet you." Childers extended his hand.

"You say this fool is one of your favorite citizens?" Longarm asked.

"I was being facetious. But he is one of my regulars. I really ought to start locking him up on Saturday mornings. Save us both a lot of trouble on Saturday nights."

"One of those."

"One of several," Childers said. "I don't suppose you federal boys have to put up with drunks like that."

"No, all we get stuck with is felons trying to shoot us. We don't generally have to wrestle them down when they're drunk." He looked at the prisoner, who was now sitting more or less upright, cold mud soaking his trousers and plenty more of it beginning to dry on his face and in his hair.

"Yeah, but that's why you get the big money, right? Dead-easy work is what I say." Childers's expression remained matter-of-fact, but his eyes betrayed the irony and sense of good humor in his statement.

"Ayuh," Longarm agreed. "Dead easy."

"What d'you want me to do with Johnny here?"

"Let's lock him up while he's still nice an' groggy. Then I'll fill out some paperwork on the charges. They oughta be enough to put him behind bars for six months or so. Couple years if I can get the right judge to hear the case." He assumed—hoped—this Johnny fella was listening.

"You take that side. I'll get this arm," Childers suggested.

"Is there a horse trough or something where we can dunk him on the way? That would wash off some of the mud so it doesn't get all over your cell." With the approach of evening, the air had turned damned well cold. Being wet with the mud was bad enough, but if Johnny were immersed, the fellow would likely take pneumonia and die. As Longarm understood quite well.

"Unfortunately, the jail is close," Childers said, "and the town well isn't. We'll take him like he is."

"Marshal Dave?" It was the big-eyed kid again.

"What is it now, Willy?"

"That horse there, sir. It's trying to eat the paint off Mr. Ryal's seegar-store Injun. Do you want I should tie him up somewhere?"

"Sure. Take him down to the livery. Tell Doc to clean him up and feed him and put him out back in the corral."

"Are you gonna pay me a dime, Marshal Dave?"

"I'm gonna give you a kick in the butt if you ask me that again. Now go on. Scat!"

The boy did not look particularly frightened by the threat. He giggled and trotted off to capture the horse's lead rope and lead it away.

Longarm took one muddy arm and Childers the other, and between them they transported a woozy and uncomplaining prisoner to the town lockup.

"I'm gonna kill your ass," the awake, aware, and once-again-belligerent miscreant declared from behind his cell bars.

"You heard that, Dave?"

"I heard it," the town marshal confirmed.

Longarm swiveled his head around to fix John Thyman with a look of unconcealed warning. "That's a separate charge of threatening a federal peace office. You want to try for five to ten? Keep talking; I'll keep writing."

"Fuck you."

"You had your chance at me. Now shut up."

"I want bail. Dammit, Dave, you got to let me out on bail. I know the rules. You got to give me bail."

"Fifty dollars," Childers said.

"Now dammit, you emptied my pockets. You know I don't got but fifteen dollars to my name."

"Eleven," the marshal corrected.

"I had. . . ."

"Fees and charges, Johnny. Including sending those clothes out to be washed. Supper. Breakfast come tomorrow. You're down to eleven dollars as it stands, and I expect that will be gone in a couple more days."

"You're a son of a bitch, Dave. You know that, don't you."

"What I know is that you aren't going anyplace without you pay fifty dollars in bail money, that's what I know."

"Then fuck you too, Dave."

"Hey, Thyman," said Longarm.

"What is it that you want, asshole?"

"That horse you were beating on. It looks like a pretty good animal. Is it yours?"

"What is this shit? Now you're trying to accuse me of stealing a horse?"

"For you, Thyman, I'd be willing to spring the trapdoor myself an' stretch your ugly neck. But that isn't what I had in mind."

"It's his horse," Childers said. "More's the pity. Not that Johnny there could ever afford a fine mount like that. But I happen to know that he drew to an inside straight, idiot that he is, and got his card. He won the horse off Charles Roberts last Saturday night. Roberts was bitching to me about it Sunday morning. Wanted me to find some reason why losing it was illegal. Roberts, you should understand, is about as much of a weasel as old Johnny there."

"Fuck you, Dave."

"Don't you ever get tired of being a prick, Johnny? Never mind. Don't answer that. It's the only thing you're good at, so how could you bear to give it up."

"I have a thought," Longarm said. "You there. Shit-for-brains. Do you want out of here while you're waiting for a court date?"

"Hell, yes, I do. But I don't got no damn fifty dollars bail money."

"Tell you what then. I'll put up the fifty."

"What?"

"Sell me that horse for fifty dollars, and I'll pay it over as bail money."

"That horse is worth a hunnerd dollars easy."

Longarm shrugged. "Suit yourself." He went back to the charge sheets he was filling out.

"Hey, dammit. I thought we was talking here."

"And I thought we were done talking. You said you don't want to sell the horse. Fine. You don't have to."

"Johnny."

"What the hell d'you want, Dave?"

"Doc charges a dollar a day to board a horse. You want I should pay him out of the eleven you got left? Of course, when that runs out, he can put a lien on the horse and sell it for the board bill. But you do what you want."

"God *damn* you two cocksucking thieves!"

"Shut up, Johnny. We got work to do here," said Dave.

"You. Fed'r'l man."

"What is it now, Thyman?"

"Seventy-five. I'll sell you the horse for seventy-five."

"No, thanks. I made my offer. You rejected it. That's fine."

"All *right,* goddammit. Fifty dollars."

"You sure about this?"

"I said it, didn't I?"

"Let's not get into your trustworthiness, Thyman. But all right. Fifty dollars. Marshal, would you please let him out . . . no, wait a minute. Better wait until after he's signed the bill of sale. Then he can go, and I'll complete his paperwork while you write up the bail."

"You do know, don't you, that you can't leave the county," Childers said to Thyman. "You'll have to be here when they notify you of a court date."

"That will be down in Denver," said Longarm. "But we'll provide your transportation there. Comes time for your appearance, you'll just report here to Dave. We'll send a deputy to escort you down to stand before the judge on these charges."

"I know how it works, dammit."

"Sure have a mouth on you, Thyman."

"Fuck you."

Longarm winked at Dave Childers and went back to the papers.

Twenty minutes later, after the bill of sale was signed and Thyman was gone, eleven dollars in his pocket and a scowl on his face, the town marshal asked, "Are you really going to file those charges in a federal court, Longarm?"

"Naw, I won't bother. But I do think I solved a problem for you. I doubt you'll see Mr. Thyman around here again. Not with him expecting a summons and a long vacation in Leavenworth."

"Want your fifty dollars back?"

"Nope. That wouldn't be fair. Pass that voucher along to your town clerk and hope the government is still solvent when he presents it for payment."

"All right. Tell me one more thing, Longarm."

"If I can."

"Want to join me while I make my rounds? I generally stop in the Snooker and Suds for a short one when I'm done prowling the alleys."

"Hell, Dave, I haven't walked night rounds in God knows how long. I'd be pleased to come along. But who buys when we get to this joint of yours?"

"A round apiece. It's the only way to be fair, don't you think?"

Childers snuffed out the flame in his desk lamp, and turned the wick low on the one that was burning on the wall. He took a sawed-off double barrel shotgun off the rack, and checked to make sure there was brass showing in both barrels, then nodded. "Ready when you are, Longarm."

Chapter 5

Longarm slept in late the next morning; the sun was already up and nearly clear of the horizon before he yawned and crawled out of bed. He enjoyed a healthy morning crap, then went downstairs for a breakfast cooked to order with the eggs just as he liked them and a bountiful display of fried spuds, fresh biscuits, and bacon gravy. No bacon, but that was all right; the gravy was good enough.

Once that was done he had to . . . do nothing. The coach wouldn't leave until the next dawn, and there was not a single thing he had to do here in the meantime. The feeling was a strange one. Idleness was not his habit.

He went outside and contemplated the rocking chairs lined up on the front porch. Only one was occupied, by an elderly man with tobacco stains in his beard and a look about him that suggested he was probably a doddering imbecile. Or in training to become one at the very least. Longarm did not relish the idea of being trapped in a long-winded and pointless conversation with him.

"G'morning, sir," Longarm said with a polite smile, however. He didn't want to spend the morning as the old goat's entertainment, but he did not want to be rude either.

"Say wha'?" The fellow cupped a hand to his ear. "Wha'd you say, son?" he shouted.

Perfect, Longarm thought. Not only senile, but deaf too. Longarm smiled again and waved to the elderly man. Waved good-bye, that is. He did not even pause on the porch long enough to light an after-meal cheroot, but waited to do that until he was around the corner.

The mud in the streets must have frozen overnight. It was thawed again now, but was even more slick and slippery than it had been the previous evening. Longarm slipped and almost fell twice just getting across the street to the board sidewalk opposite.

He ambled over to the business district, and found a barbershop that had three other customers ahead of him. Not that he was in a hurry. He reread a copy of yesterday's *Rocky Mountain News,* and by the time he was done with that was next in line for the chair.

"Haircut, mister?"

"Just a shave, thanks."

"You could use a trim there."

"Just a shave, thanks."

"How about some cologne when I'm done."

"Just a shave, thanks."

The barber gave up trying to earn a little extra profit off the stranger, and settled for the shave only. Longarm thanked him.

Longarm walked down to the livery and looked in to see that his new horse was being taken care of. It was. Not only had it been fed and watered, the mud had been brushed off it, along with much of the loose hair from the past winter's coat. Now that it was cleaned up, it was a damned fine-looking animal, a blood bay with three white stockings and a snip above the muzzle. It had wide-set forelegs, broad hips, and shoulder bones at a nearly perfect forty-five-degree angle; its trot likely would be a pleasure to sit after some of the bone-jarring hammerheads the Army wound up with.

"You do good work," Longarm said, complimenting the liveryman, whose name, predictably enough since he would probably also serve as the local veterinary, was Doc.

"He's a good horse," said Doc, "Worth a mite o' extra trouble. I grained him good too, and went heavy on the hot feed."

That would likely be expensive, Longarm knew. "Nobody's raising corn around here, are they?" he asked.

Doc shrugged. "That's what God invented trains for, ain't it?"

"Well, I appreciate it." Longarm paid the man an extra dollar, and gave him a government voucher to cover the normal boarding expenses.

He would have been satisfied to stay and visit there for a while, but Doc was busy with his morning routines, and more importantly, by then Longarm was wanting another cheroot, and smoking is not generally welcome inside a barn, certainly not inside someone else's barn.

Longarm thanked Doc again and wandered back onto the streets. This idleness wasn't all it was cracked up to be.

He tipped his Stetson to a woman who was crossing the street toward him. It didn't feel particularly cold to him, but she was bundled up so deep in hat, cloak collar, and muff that he could see little more than her nose and eyes peeping out past the fringe of fur on the hat that framed her face. "Ma'am." He wasn't sure, but got the impression that she might have smiled in return, although she said nothing to him.

As she came near, she slipped in the mud and one foot flew completely out from under her.

Longarm instinctively grasped her elbow to steady her and keep her from falling into the cold mud.

"Oh! I . . . forgive me, sir. I'm terribly clumsy. Thank you very much. I . . ."

"You son of a *bitch*!"

Longarm knew without having to look that John Thyman hadn't fled Rawlins after all. Yet. Miserable bastard.

Longarm looked behind him in time to see a sunburst of flame encircle the muzzle of Thyman's revolver. A bullet sizzled past close to Longarm's ear.

His first thought was for the woman who was caught in the line of fire and was every bit as exposed to the bullets as Longarm was.

He swept her up and whirled, throwing her shoulder-high through the air for a good eight or ten feet.

Thyman had time to shoot twice more while Longarm was busy trying to get the innocent bystander out of harm's way.

Once that was accomplished, however, Longarm was free to devote his attention to the disgruntled Mr. Thyman.

Thyman fired one final time, and a gout of mud spurted geyser-like from the street as his slug went wildly astray.

But then perhaps he saw that he'd missed, and in his last moments had time to realize what was certain to happen next.

Longarm's Colt roared, the backstrap pushing hard into the web of his hand. The bullet struck Thyman about four inches above his belt buckle, doubling him over at the waist even more effectively than Longarm's punch had done the day before.

Not one to take unnecessary chances with someone who wanted to kill him, Longarm took careful aim and fired twice more.

Thyman dropped onto the sidewalk. He would not be moving again, not under-his own power anyway.

Longarm shoved the .44 back into his holster and hurried over to see if the woman had been harmed.

Chapter 6

The woman gave no sign of life when Longarm bent over her. He looked up to see several people staring out from the safety of store doorways. "Is there a doctor here?" he called. "And somebody . . . you there . . . go find Marshal Childers. You. Tell me where I can find your doc. Don't just stand there gawking, dammit. Help me."

While he was barking instructions, Longarm scooped the unconscious woman into his arms. He stood, carefully balancing in the mud so he didn't dump her back into it, while a man in sleeve garters and an eyeshade gave directions to the doctor's office. Around the corner and two blocks up. Longarm cradled the woman tight to his chest and walked carefully to the secure footing on the sidewalk, then took off at a slow trot. He did not want to jostle the girl any more than he had to. But at the same time he wanted to get her to the doctor as quickly as possible. He had no idea where she was shot, and did not want to stop to look for any wounds beneath the heavy cloak.

He was almost to the doctor's office when he felt her stir in his arms. Her eyelashes fluttered and a moment later she came fully awake. "Sir, I . . . where are you taking me? Stop. Please, stop."

He did, afraid the movement was too much for her. But there was no pain in her voice or expression, only puzzlement, and that quickly passed.

"Put me down. Please."

"You need medical care, miss. Where . . . uh . . . I don't mean t' be personal, ma'am, but where're you hit?"

"Hit? Oh. Shot, you mean. I . . . I don't believe I have been shot."

"But I thought . . ."

She shook her head. "I may have swooned. But just for a moment. The excitement . . . it was awful. Truly awful. That man was trying to kill you, wasn't he, sir?" She shuddered.

"Yes, ma'am, I s'pose he was. But don't you worry. It's all right now. He won't be botherin' you again."

"Did you . . . did you shoot him?"

"Yes, ma'am."

"How awful."

"Not when y' think o' the alternative," he answered with a smile.

"No, I suppose not. Uh, sir."

"Yes, miss?"

"You can put me down now. Really."

"Oh. I kinda forgot." The smile returned. "T' tell you the truth, I was kinda hoping you'd forget too. I got to admit you're nice t' hold onto."

She was too. Her hat had fallen off, and dangled now from the yarn ties that were secured at her throat. And a very pretty throat it was too. Along with the face that was now visible.

Longarm guessed she was in her very early twenties. She still had the flawless complexion and smooth, taut flesh of youth. Her eyes were large, a soft brown lightly flecked with gold and . . . green? He could not decide about that. Her cheeks were round, and she had dimples at the corners of a wide, expressive mouth.

In ten years, he knew, she would be plain and time-worn. Today she had the freshness of youth to bolster her appearance.

She was slender. He could tell that because she weighed practically nothing in his arms.

"Sir?"

"What? Oh!" Longarm felt heat rush to his cheeks and ears. He was still standing there on the public streets of Rawlins, Wyoming Territory, holding her as if he didn't want to let go.

Come to think of it, he was in no hurry at all to put her down.

"Are you sure you feel all right, miss?"

"Yes, thank you."

Carefully he bent a little and set her onto her feet. "Hold onto my arm now in case you get woozy again."

She looked at him, and seemed to realize what effect her closeness was having on him. She smiled. "Would you do something for me?"

"Of course."

"Please escort me home."

"Are you sure I can't take you t' the doc's office?"

"No. Please, no."

"Marshal?"

Longarm turned to see one of the townspeople on the corner nearby. "What is it?"

"Marshal Childers is looking for you, Marshal."

"Tell Dave I'll be along to fill out his reports directly."

"Yes, sir, Marshal."

Longarm returned his attention to the girl. "It'd be best if you let the doc look at you, miss."

"No!" she snapped, a sharp edge in her voice. She was, he realized, fearful of being seen by the doctor, despite the ordeal of barely escaping that asshole Thyman's bullets.

"All right. No need t' get worked up about it. I'll take you home. You want me t' carry you?"

"That won't be necessary. Really."

"All right, but if you start feeling wobbly, you let me know."

"I will. I promise."

"Fine. Now take hold o' my arm an' tell me where we're going."

Her name was Amanda, and she lived in a room above the carriage shed of a large and quite elegant home just outside the Rawlins business district. She did not say so, but Longarm guessed she was a housemaid in the residence or had some similar employment there.

Longarm helped her up a flight of steep, very narrow steps and inside. He stopped in the doorway there and removed his Stetson. "Are you sure you're all right now, miss?"

"I'm fine. Thank you."

"In that case, I better be going. Uh, be careful of that cloak o' yours. It's pretty muddy."

"Oh, dear. It is, isn't it? It looks like I've been rolling in a hog wallow."

"You have. Or the next thing to it."

"Yes, I suppose I did at that. Oh, my. And look at your poor coat. You've gotten all muddy too from carrying me."

Longarm shrugged. "I'll see can I find a place t' get it cleaned." He smiled. "That'll give me something t' do today."

"I won't hear of it. Close the door, please, and take that coat off. I can clean it for you."

"You don't have t' do that, miss."

"Perhaps so, but I certainly want to. After all, I do owe

you my life. Did that man say you are a marshal?"

Longarm introduced himself.

"Gracious. And a very gallant gentleman too. Now come in. Please. Take that coat off and let me take care of it for you. I know just what to do. Now give it to me. I shall hang it here and let it dry a while so I can brush it and then clean it properly. Sit down. Over there, please."

Not that there were all that many places to choose from. The room held only one chair, a curtained-off area to serve as a wardrobe, a bed, and a sheet-metal sheepherder's stove. She had made curtains out of flour sacking, and set a discarded crate beside the stove to serve as a cupboard. Apparently she did not do any cooking here, but she had a small teapot and a bucket of water.

Longarm occupied the chair. Amanda opened a window despite the cool morning and hung his coat in front of it to dry. The sleeves, he had to admit, were very badly in need of cleaning after he'd carried her.

She gave her cloak a rueful look—it really was quite filthy, much more so than Longarm's coat—and hung that over the other window.

With the two garments blocking both windows, the interior of her room was dim, the lighting making it seem more intimate.

"Now," she said, "I shall put water on for tea. And we can wait for your coat to dry."

She did not seem at all uncomfortable with the thought of entertaining a stranger in the privacy of her living quarters.

Chapter 7

Longarm was not entirely sure how it happened. One moment she was bending over him with a teaspoon of sugar to drop into the tea she handed him. And the next second the tea was forgotten, the sugar had been spilled, and the girl was in his lap with her face only fractions of an inch in front of his.

He kissed her. It seemed a natural and proper thing to do under the circumstances.

She tasted of . . . cloves? As if she'd been chewing cloves. He was fairly sure of it. Didn't mind it either. In fact, he went back for another taste just to be sure. And another after that.

Amanda moaned softly and curled one arm behind his neck. She didn't have to worry about holding him in place. He wasn't going anywhere.

"Nice," she whispered, her lips moving softly on his mouth. Her tongue flirted with his, and she began to stroke his cheek and the side of his neck with her free hand.

"Amanda."

"Yes?"

"There's somethin' you ought t' know."

"Yes, dear?"

"We either got t' quit this or move on to somethin', well, somethin' more serious. You know what I mean?"

She giggled. And began unfastening the buttons on his vest and on the shirt beneath it.

That was all the encouragement Longarm needed. He reached for the buttons at her throat. "No," she whispered. "Let me do this."

Ever a gentleman, Custis Long let the little lady have her way. It seemed the decent thing to do.

She unbuttoned everything she could reach, then slipped off his lap so she could finish the job, removing, carefully folding, and then laying aside his garments one by one. The gunbelt she did let him take care of, while she knelt to wipe his boots and then tug them off. Damned considerate of her, he thought.

When he was naked, she took him by the hand and urged him onto his feet. Led him to the sturdy bed that dominated the small room. She took the blanket off and folded it before placing it carefully onto the chair they had just vacated. She peeled the sheet back and helped him under it.

"May I ask a favor of you?" she said.

"You c'n ask, sure."

"Turn your head. I . . . I know this sounds silly. But I don't want you to see me nude. I . . . I feel shy of a sudden. Would you do that? Please?"

Shy. Yeah, sure. Longarm managed to keep from laughing. But it wasn't easy.

Still, if it made the girl feel better for it, what the hell. He turned his head aside and peered at the cups and spoons and very few other articles arranged in her makeshift cupboard.

Behind him he could hear the rustle of cloth. The light in the room faded, so he guessed she was pulling the flour-sack draperies over the windows. Then more rustling suggested she was removing her clothing. A moment later he felt the side of the bed sag and the touch of cool, bare skin against his back. He rolled over and took her into his arms.

Amanda had drawn the sheet to her throat. He could not see her body, but he could certainly feel it. He conducted his explorations manually.

She was thin almost to the point of emaciation. He could feel her shoulders and collarbone sharp beneath the softness of skin. Her breasts were small and unusually firm, the nipples very hard and also quite small. He cupped and teased them for several moments, then allowed his hand to slip lower.

"Please," she said, taking his wrist and moving his hand on down to the puffy softness that guarded her pubis. "Touch me there. Please," she whispered.

Longarm searched within the curly forest, and found the opening already moist and receptive. He gently probed her body, and once his fingertips were thoroughly wet, pulled out again to rub small circles over and around the tiny rosebud of her pleasure. Amanda began to moan, her hips rising and falling to his touch.

"Are you ready?" she asked, her voice hoarse and cracking.

"Um-hmm."

"Now. Let me feel you inside me now, please."

He complied, rising to his knees and moving over her.

Amanda spread her knees apart and grasped his waist. Greedily, she pulled him down onto her.

And into her.

Longarm entered her as if his cock had a mind of its own and already knew the way home. Her flesh was hot and damp and surrounded him with a hard upward thrust of her hips.

Amanda gasped and her eyes went wide as she felt the

length of his hard shaft. She began to smile and then gaily, joyously to laugh.

Longarm too smiled. He kissed her, taking his time about it, and only then began the slow thrust and retreat that soon would accelerate into a frenzy of pounding lust.

Chapter 8

Longarm groaned and spread his thighs a little further apart so Amanda could cup his balls in her hands and lightly tickle them. She was already in that neighborhood, busily sucking him back to life after several previous ejaculations. Amanda, it seemed, was a very lusty lady.

Actually, Longarm would have been happy to take a breather for a little while. It was getting on toward lunchtime, and his belly was beginning to rumble . . . he wondered how that sounded from down where she now was . . . and he would have liked a smoke too. They'd been going at it hot and heavy for quite a while now.

Still, it would have been rude if he were to grab her ears and hoist her off his pole. He let her keep going, the pleasure of it accompanied by the sounds of Amanda's vigorous slurping and gobbling.

Her purpose was certainly achieved, he acknowledged, as the blind snake was once again standing to attention.

Amanda lifted her pretty face from him and asked, "I can feel . . . you're close to coming again, aren't you?"

"Uh-huh. I wouldn't've thought it, but . . . uh-huh."

"I don't like the taste of come in my mouth. Do you mind, honey, if I ask you to come in my pussy instead?"

"Fine by me. Tell you what. Just kinda slide up onta my belly there an' jab yourself where it feels the best."

"You want me on top?"

"Sure, why not."

She giggled, then clambered up his belly and chest, climbing him like a squirrel scampering up a tall oak tree until she was on top of him. She sat upright and raised herself a bit, allowing Longarm's already wet and eager cock to find the furry opening and slide once again inside her body.

Amanda leaned back, her eyelids drooping as the sensation of being so thoroughly filled by his hot shaft overcame her. "God, honey, you're so big. I just naturally do love this."

Longarm didn't exactly object to it either.

The sheet she had been so intent on covering herself with was forgotten for a moment, and slipped off her shoulders to fall across his knees. Longarm was able to see her fully for the first time.

He liked what he saw. Full lips. Slender neck. Prominent collarbone. Firm pink titties with nipples the size and color of raisins. Waist that was . . .

He blinked and looked again.

Waist that was amazingly thick for such a small girl. And a tummy that was as round as a small melon.

So *that* was what she'd been trying to hide.

"Hey!" he said.

"What, sweetie?"

"Are you sure this is safe?"

Amanda opened her eyes and looked at him. She seemed puzzled. "You don't like it?"

"You know I like it. But won't . . . uh . . . won't this . . . well . . . can't it hurt the . . . you know." He motioned with his chin to indicate the rounded belly. "Can't doing this hurt the kid you're carrying."

Amanda gave out a yelp and grabbed for the missing

sheet, but it was much too late for that to hide anything now. She started to cry.

Longarm pulled her down on top of him and wrapped his arms around her. He was still buried deep inside her, but with this distraction could feel himself begin to go limp. Eventually he shrank enough that the now-flaccid member slid gently out of her, the relative chill of the air cool against that bit of wet, exposed flesh.

Amanda did not seem to notice. She was busy crying and leaking snot onto Longarm's shoulder.

He stroked her hair and patted her back and tried to soothe her as best he could. "There, there now. It's all right." A thought occurred to him and he asked, "Is that why you were so set against goin' t' see the doc a little while ago?"

Her reply was an indistinct whimper and snuffle, but he could feel her nod her head against his chest and took that to mean yes.

"Nobody knows? Not even your folks?"

"I . . . I . . . I'm an orphan, L . . . L . . . Longarm honey. I don't have any family."

"What about the people you work for?"

"Th . . . th . . . that's who knocked me up," she wailed, and went into another bout of intense weeping that deposited a whole fresh bucket of nose-drip onto him.

Longarm patted her somewhat awkwardly. The snot was kind of messy. And it didn't feel all that grand once it was commencing to cool. He pulled up a corner of the sheet and used that to wipe most of it away, then peered at the patch of wet cloth and marveled. Who the hell would've thought there could be that much snot in such a small girl. It was true, though; a fella learns something every day.

"I . . . I . . . I'm so ashamed," Amanda bawled. She pressed her face against him and let loose another torrent of snot and tears. "I don't know wh . . . what to do. H . . .

h . . . he raped me. I didn't want him to fuck me. H . . . h . . . he's old and h . . . h . . . he's ugly, and I told him I didn't want to. But h . . . h . . . he grabbed me and h . . . h . . . he forced me. M . . . m . . . most every day, he did that. H . . . h . . . his wife would g . . . g . . . go out to shop and h . . . h . . . he would find me and r . . . r . . . rape me. I never wanted him t . . . t . . . to do that. And now I'm pre . . . pre . . . pregnant and I don't know what to d . . . d . . . do."

The sobbing intensified. She kept on telling him something, but she was crying so hard Longarm could not understand what she was saying.

"R . . . r . . . rape ought to b . . . b . . . be against the law. It r . . . r . . . really should."

"Did you tell Marshal Childers about any of this, Amanda? Rape is a very serious offense, you know."

"I . . . I . . . no, I d . . . d . . . didn't."

"Why not?"

"The m . . . m . . . marshal is a f . . . f . . . friend of his. He w . . . w . . . wouldn't believe me, I know he w . . . w . . . wouldn't."

"But you don't really know that since you didn't report the rapes, isn't that so?" Longarm said.

She stopped crying for a moment and lifted her head. Her eyes were puffy and red now, and a long string of snot ran from her left nostril into Longarm's chest hair. Funny thing, but she didn't look quite so pretty at the moment. Nor so desirable. Longarm figured they were definitely done screwing now.

"D . . . d . . . did that man outside say you're a m . . . m . . . marshal too?"

"Uh-huh. Deputy United States marshal actually."

"Could y . . . y . . . you arrest him? M . . . m . . . make him take care of his b . . . b . . . *baby*?" Amanda dissolved into a bawling, howling heap at that, and pushed her face hard against Longarm's chest again.

Longarm sighed. Wiping off wasn't going to be nearly enough. He was going to have to go back to the barbershop and this time pay for a bath. Oh, well. At least that would give the barber a little more profit for the day and make him happy. It would be good if somebody turned out to get some pleasure from this, Longarm thought.

But thinking that was unkind of him, wasn't it. Amanda had given him plenty of pleasure. Right up until now. He should be grateful to her for that.

He sighed again, and steeled himself to do his duty and let her tell him the whole sordid tale.

He just hoped he could get her to get off him while she talked. Sitting elsewhere with a pail under her chin to catch all the fluids would be good. At the very least, maybe he could get her to roll over so she would moisten the pillow instead of him.

"Tell me all about it," he said, taking her by the shoulders and gently rolling her off him and down onto the bed at his side.

But he kept hold of the sheet to towel off with.

Chapter 9

"Hmm, yes, that is a very serious charge indeed," Dave Childers agreed. "I can see how you would want to get Harold to take care of your baby."

"His baby," Amanda corrected.

"Right. Yours and his together," the town marshal amended. "Do you want him locked up in the state pen too? Or just ordered to pay for the child's well-being?"

"I . . . I hadn't thought of that, Marshal."

"Uh-huh. Well I'll tell you what. Federal law supercedes state or local law in these matters, so I may turn this case over to my friend Longarm here and let him take it to the federal courts down in Denver."

"What would that mean, sir?"

"For one thing, it would mean you would receive a much larger award if the judge found in your favor. You see, our little local courts don't have all the power that the federal courts do. Of course you would have to go to Denver when the case comes up for hearing. Might even have to move there. These things can take an awful long time in the federal court system. Isn't that right, Longarm?"

Longarm had no idea just what game Dave was playing, but he figured the man was sure to have a good reason. "That's right, Marshal. Court proceedings can take a terrible long time."

"I wouldn't mind moving there," Amanda said. "But I don't have any money. Would he have to pay me something while I'm waiting for my award?"

"I expect we would have to see about that, Amanda," Childers said solemnly. "Now do us a favor, would you? I need to speak with Marshal Long in private. Law things, don't you see. So I would like you to go home and go about your regular duties this afternoon. Just don't tell Harold what you're up to. Can you do that for us, please?"

The girl bounced to her feet, all smiles and eagerness. "Yes, sir, Marshal Dave." She headed toward the door, then paused there. "Do you think I should start to pack now?"

"I think that would be a very good idea, Amanda."

The girl was downright bubbly when she left.

Longarm turned to Childers with a raised eyebrow. "Dave . . ." Childers should know quite as well as Longarm did that there were no paternity issues written into federal law. Any judge on the federal bench would demand Longarm's badge—and damn well get it—if he were to bring an issue like this before him.

"I know, I know. Give me one of those little cigars of yours, would you? Those are tasty."

Childers waited until he and Longarm had their cheroots trimmed and lighted before he offered an explanation. Then he leaned back in his swivel chair and said, "There's some things your little Amanda doesn't know, Longarm. But I do. And I probably wouldn't know either if Harold wasn't married to my aunt.

"First off, Amanda is no innocent country girl forced to make her own way in a cold, cruel world. One of the things that I happen to know, you see, is that she's no orphan. Her family lives over in Nebraska. Her pa kicked her out when she got to whoring around and"—he stopped and waved his hand—"no, that isn't fair for me to say. Far as I know, she never took money for it. But she was lifting her skirt for a spell before she ever came here. I can guess how she paid her train fare to get this far. Then Harold's wife Edith took pity on her and gave her that job as a housekeeper.

"Harold, by the way, is probably the richest man in Rawlins. Are you beginning to make some sense out of this now, Custis?"

"Could be. But a girl having easy virtue don't mean a man shouldn't meet his responsibilities to her. Keep talking."

"Oh, I agree with you. Very much so, in fact. The way I see, it a man is responsible for his own actions whatever they are, good or bad."

"We got no disagreement there, Dave."

"Right. So mayhap you'll want to know that Amanda has a couple boyfriends in town here. Nothing serious. She just likes to fuck. But any one of those randy youngsters could be the papa of that kid she's carrying."

"I'm listening."

"As for Harold, he couldn't be."

"She's a pretty enough little thing, Dave, and the most respectable man can find himself in temptation's way sometimes. Why, I've known more than a few preachers to get carried away and find themselves with some girl's skirt lifted and the padre's pants down around his ankles without he ever consciously intends for it t' happen. You likely know of such things your own self."

"Oh, indeed I do," Childers agreed. "But if you'll recall, I did mention that Harold is married to my aunt. So I know a few little things that aren't talked about outside the family. One of those things is that when Harold was a captain of artillery with the 12th Ohio in the recent conflict, a sliver of Confederate shrapnel came close to killing him. It cut into his groin. Right down about here. And apart from damn near causing him to bleed to death, that exploding shell cut off Harold's balls. Around here everybody marvels that he always keeps himself so tidy and neat, always looks fresh shaved. Longarm, he hasn't had a beard to need shaving since a couple years after the war ended. So you see, I really don't think it likely that Harold is the one who fathered that child. He's just the one close by who could best come up with money to support Amanda."

"I know you'll be needing me to make out a report for you about the Thyman shooting," Longarm said, dropping the one subject in favor of something of more interest, "but could we do that after lunch? I'm hungry as a bear with six cubs. Hell, I'll even buy lunch for us both, courtesy of Uncle Sam."

"I know just the place. Get your hat and follow me."

Chapter 10

A stagecoach with relays of fresh horses waiting every so many miles would have made it a helluva lot quicker, but one man mounted on one horse could only travel so far even if the horse was a mighty good one. Which Longarm's new mount most certainly was.

The animal did not just look good, it performed even better than it looked. It had the easy trot that its bone structure promised—well, relatively easy, any trot being by nature a sonuvabitch on the rider but easy on the mount—and to Longarm's delight it had a long striding road gait that was as smooth as one of those plantation horses that came out of Tennessee.

With the horse in that extended walk, Longarm was able to cover ground at the rate of five or six miles each hour and do it in as much comfort as if he'd been lounging in a parlor chair. It seemed a damn shame that he had no need for a personally owned horse—nothing prevented him from owning and paying board for one except common sense—or he would redeem that fifty-dollar voucher himself and keep the animal. Longarm figured that simple-minded asshole John Thyman had undervalued the horse when he said it was worth a hundred dollars.

From Rawlins Longarm rode south on the road to Baggs, and spent a night there in a narrow and lumpy bed. At least that one had no little bitty livestock wandering around in the mattress straw like the bed he hired the next night in Meeker. That one was so thoroughly populated with bedbugs that Longarm gave up on it after an hour and a half or so and went outside to finish the night sleeping in the hayloft over the stable.

He reached the Colorado River at Hooper's Ferry the third day, and paid an outrageous fee—half a damn dollar, but it was either pay that or find your own way over—to reach the south bank. Rather than pay the highwayman who ran the ferry station another four dollars—*four*, mind—to board man and beast for a single night—*one* night, mind—Longarm chose to sleep in his own bedroll with the stars for a ceiling.

From there it was an easy day and a half on to Weirville in Hart County so he could set about the business Billy Vail had sent him out on.

Which, the way he saw it, would be nothing more than making a show of his presence so the political hacks would see and be happy. The whole thing was a useless waste of time, Longarm figured. But Billy had no choice about it and therefore neither did he, so his best course would be to grit his teeth and get it the hell done with.

If he'd thought Rawlins was a gray and homely place, that was only because he hadn't yet seen Weirville. Rawlins was only in training to be ugly; Weirville had ugly down to an art form.

The town had only two streets, those running parallel to and on each side of the narrow creek that appeared to be the reason a town was established there. Everything else was in the form of shacks and shanties scattered haphazardly upon the sage flat that extended for miles in every direction.

As newcomers added to the community, they extended the two existing streets further up or down the creek rather than create a cohesive town structure with the normal cross streets and grid layout. At least that was what Longarm assumed. The twin creek-side streets that comprised Weirville were about a mile and a half long, although often with a good bit of space separating one building from another. The population could not possibly have been large enough to justify so large an area otherwise.

There were half-a-dozen or so bridges linking the two sides, even though nowhere along the length of it did the creek flow more than hock-deep on a small horse. The bridges were there for wagons, he supposed. And women. Kids would almost certainly prefer to charge back and forth amid splashing and shouting . . . and hope to dry off afterward before their mothers called them in and found out. Longarm got a smile out of that thought. But then he'd been a kid once too.

That, however, had been some little time back, and there wouldn't be any splashing in the creek this trip.

Before anything else, he rode the length of the northernmost street, crossed the creek, and rode back again on its southern twin.

The north side held the saloons, a gaming hall, a sprawling ramshackle mess made partially of adobe and partially from basket-woven willow withes plastered over with mud—he guessed that would be a whorehouse because there was plenty of corral space adjacent to it—and businesses like a barber, saddler, bootmaker, blacksmith, livery/stage-line agent, hardware, general mercantile, and the like.

The southern street had a more refined collection of businesses like the church, millinery, cratery—whatever the hell that was; that was what the sign said—eateries—he knew what those were—the haberdashery, another general mercantile—this one advertising a post office contract station inside—a small bank, and the Hart County courthouse, with a clutch of lawyers' offices tucked in tight around it, no doubt so the vultures could perch there and be ready to swoop in whenever they smelled blood in the air.

The courthouse was made of stone and was the only two-story structure in the town. There were no pillars and no colonnade, but to make up for that the county fathers had put a domed cupola on top of the building, and aped the State Capitol by somehow gilding the dome and the figure of Blind Justice that sat at its peak.

Longarm might have been more impressed with the courthouse if there hadn't been a pair of goats tethered on stakes in front of it, trying to make a living on the few sprigs of grass that grew there.

According to Billy Vail, the problems here resulted from a split between two political factions. But Billy didn't know, and therefore could not explain, who all these folks were and why they were split apart.

Longarm did know for openers that at least one county commissioner was in opposition to the county sheriff. But where the other town and county officials stood, neither Billy nor Longarm had any clue.

His first order of business, Longarm decided, probably should be to find himself a place to stay while he was here—it occurred to him that he hadn't spotted a hotel during his tour of Weirville—and then go get himself a haircut.

There is nothing like a barber chair when it comes to the gathering of information in a strange town.

Chapter 11

"Looks like you could use a shave today too, mister."

"Just a trim, thanks."

"Wouldn't be much extra for a shave."

"Just the trim, thank you."

"Right. So what was it you was asking?" The barber loudly snapped his scissors in the air half-a-dozen times or more, then began lifting sprigs of hair with a comb and snipping them off. Longarm's observation was that all barbers liked to snap at thin air a few times before cutting any hair; he never had figured out why.

"A place to stay," Longarm said. "There's no hotel and if there's boardinghouses, I haven't spotted any signs."

"Nope, no hotel. Got plenty of boardinghouses, though."

"Where are they?"

The barber laughed. "All around you. Pretty much any house close to the street will take in boarders, you see. That's kind of the way we are here. Just pick a place that looks likely, then you knock and ask. Generally only one or two rooms to let, you see. If those are already full, they'll send you on to the next place." He snapped his scissors again, then resumed cutting. "Comes from this being such a hardscrabble piece of country. Especially was in the early days, though not quite so much so now. Nobody was making much money then, so everybody was willing to take in a guest or two to help make ends meet. Take folks in and treat them like as if they was family.

"It's become . . . I don't know that you'd call it a tradition. But nearly everybody still does it. Which is why there's no hotel. We got folks coming through pretty regular, but they're already tended to with the boarding. Wouldn't be business enough for a hotel, you see. And then there's the fact that if somebody was to come in and build a hotel and take away all the extra income, he'd be one unpopular son of a bitch." The man stopped cutting and came toward the front of the chair a step so he could peer closely at Longarm. "You wasn't thinking to start a hotel here, was you?"

Longarm smiled. "No, friend, I don't have any notion to open a hotel here. Or anyplace else, for that matter."

"That's good. Wouldn't want the whole town down on you."

"You wouldn't happen to have a recommendation about where I could put up, would you?" Longarm asked.

"Which side of the town are you doing business with?" the barber countered.

"Pardon? I don't think I understand what you're asking."

"North or south?"

"During the war, you mean?"

"No, not during no damn war. Business. Which side of the town are you wanting to do business on. That's part of our habit too. A man always stays on the side of town where he wants to do business. Keeps from making anybody mad on that side, and it doesn't do much hurt to make the other side mad, you see."

"Actually, I don't see," Longarm admitted.

"You don't see why you wouldn't want to get your own

clients or customers or whoever mad at you?"

"I don't see what the different sides of town have to do with anything."

"You really don't?"

"I thought I said that."

The barber smeared a little shaving cream onto the nape of Longarm's neck and used a razor to scrape away the short hairs there, then spread some of the remaining lather with the ball of his thumb and tidied up Longarm's sideburns. He brought out a pair of very small, very sharp scissors and began snipping at the fringes of Longarm's mustache.

"Not too much there, please."

"I'm just shaping it a little. Won't make it shorter."

"All right."

"What was I saying?"

"About the two sides of town," Longarm reminded him.

"Oh, yes. That. It's pretty simple. North side of the creek is the sheep crowd. South is the fruit growers and dirt farmers. One side don't have much to do with the other, you see."

"The courthouse is on the north side," Longarm observed.

"The sheep men was here years before the farmers moved in."

"And you're on the south side."

The barber smiled. "I'm also the only barber in town. Also as close as we got to having a doctor seeing as how I graduated back East as a fully qualified barber surgeon. And I'm the undertaker too. Folks tend to make an exception for me, you see. They never know when they'll need my services. Or which."

"Handy." So this garrulous fellow was the Weirville undertaker. Longarm was going to want some more conversation with him. Later. When he had a better idea who he should ask about and perhaps got a little better handle on what the questions should be.

"You sure you don't want a shave, mister?"

"Tomorrow," Longarm said. "I'll come back in the morning so I can start the day with a fresh shave."

The barber made a sour face. "Everybody thinks that same way. Makes me busy as a one-armed juggler every morning and fair puts me to sleep in the afternoons. I'd be a happier man if I could talk half my customers into getting their shaves in the afternoons."

"It's hard to change human nature," Longarm said.

"Tell me about it."

"So anyway," Longarm said, returning to the previous subject, "if I take a room on this side of the creek, everyone will think I'm siding with the farmers and the sheepmen won't trust me. But if I sleep on the north side, then the farmers won't want anything to do with me and the sheepmen will assume I'm with them. Is that about it?"

"In a nutshell, yes." The barber stepped back a pace, scowled, and gave his chair a critical walk-around. Finally he nodded, satisfied with the job he'd done. He poured a dash of Pinaud Clubman into his palm and rubbed his hands together, then smoothed the scent onto the back of Longarm's neck. He didn't ask if Longarm wanted it. But then he did not charge extra for it either. Obviously he was a gent who took pride in his work. Probably took pleasure in it too, Longarm judged.

"What if I ride out away a piece and sleep outside the town?"

"Then folks will think you're either daft or neutral."

"Get much rain hereabouts?"

The barber laughed. "Nope. Just make sure you stay clear of the sheep fords. The ground gets pretty thick with sheep shit around those."

"I'll keep that in mind, thanks."

"Any time, mister." He removed the neck cloth with a

flourish and snapped it to toss the bits of hair onto the floor.

Longarm stood and paid the man a well-earned two bits. "I'll see you in the morning."

"Yep. You and most everybody else in town. Tell you what, mister. Come after lunch and I'll give you a discount."

Longarm chuckled and went back outside to the horse he'd tied on the street.

Chapter 12

Sleeping out was one thing. Cooking for himself was another. Oh, he could do it adequately. But the fact was that he would rather eat someone else's worst biscuits than his own best. He led the horse up the street—the south street as he happened already to be on that side of the creek—enjoying the feeling of being able to stretch his legs after so many days in the saddle getting there.

The first café he came to looked to be a likely enough place. There were even curtains at the front window. A man didn't see that just every day, even back in Denver. He tied the horse to a nearby rail and went in, pausing at the entrance to remove his hat and look around.

He was a little early for supper or plenty late for lunch and the place was empty, except for a man in overalls who was engaged in earnest conversation with an older man wearing a suit and tie. They were at a table near the front of the place, so Longarm walked to the back and chose a table against the wall, his preferred spot anyway as it discouraged backshooters. Not that he anticipated there being any shooting on this job, but it was an old habit and in his line of work a sensible one. Hell, he could be shot at by total strangers who recognized him and because of their own guilt leaped to a false conclusion that the federal lawman was after them. It had happened more than once in the past, and could well happen again. A man just never knew, so it paid to take care.

A waitress appeared in response to the tinkling of a tiny bell that was activated whenever the front door was opened. She was as pretty a girl as Longarm could remember seeing in years, with golden blond hair, a peaches-and-cream complexion, and huge, innocent blue eyes. She was so pretty, it just made him feel good to look at her.

She was also about twelve years old, and still had freckles dusting the bridge of her nose.

"Yes, sir, what's your order?"

"D'you have a menu?"

"Naw, we always cook the same things. It's either beef stew or chicken pot pie."

"What would your recommendation be?" he asked.

"Take the pot pie. Mama makes wonderful dumplings." She giggled just a little. "And the beef is tough. But don't tell my mama that I said so. She's in a hurry to get rid of it."

"I'll have the pot pie, thanks."

"Coffee?"

"You bet."

"Supper comes with a free piece of dried apple pie. Lunch don't."

"What's the difference?"

"Five cents. Lunch is twenty cents. Supper's a quarter."

"But the pie is free," he said.

She giggled again. "That's what mama says I'm to tell folks."

Longarm laughed. He liked the kid. She was honest. She'd probably outgrow that in time. But he liked her for it and hoped she wouldn't change. "I'll have the supper in that case. But say, I thought folks around here raised fruit. How come the pie is from dried apples?"

" 'Cause there's nothing in season this early," she said patiently. "If it makes you feel any better, the apples we use were raised here."

"Much better, thanks."

"Give me just a second. I'll be back with your supper."

She was as good as her word, returning in less than a minute with a tray containing a large bowl of chicken . . . stuff. He wasn't sure if it should be called a pot pie or chicken and dumplings as it had both dumplings inside and a thin brown crust on top. In other words, it was made of mostly cheap ingredients with a lot of flour and dried vegetables and a few morsels of tender chicken. Regardless of that, it was damned good and the portion was generous. So was the slice of pie that went with it, and the coffee was excellent.

Longarm finished a thoroughly satisfying meal and placed thirty-five cents on the table, then picked up his Stetson and ambled outside for a postprandial cigar. The farmer and the gent in the suit were still huddled in intense conversation at the front.

He'd had supper on the south side of town and figured if he wanted to spread things around, as seemed to be a good idea around here, he should go over to the north side for a drink.

He untied the horse and swung onto the saddle, then put it into a slow trot toward the nearest bridge across to the sheep side of Weirville.

"I'll take three," Longarm said around the stub of a cheroot, his head cocked to one side to avoid the thin stream of aromatic smoke that rose from the little cigar.

"And the dealer takes two," a man named Jimerson said as he peeled three cards off the top of the deck and slid them over to Longarm, then removed his own two. He carefully arranged the new cards into his hand and said,

"I opened. I'll go a quarter here, gentlemen."

Two players dropped out immediately. The man on Longarm's right tossed a quarter into the pot and another dime on top of it. "Thirty-five to you, friend."

Longarm glanced at the cards he'd been given. The draw had done nothing to improve the pair of treys he'd started with. He shook his head and tossed the cards face-down into the middle of the table.

"I'll see your dime, Louie," the dealer said. He contributed to the pot and asked, "Whaddya got?"

The player named Louie scowled and said, "I shoulda gone up a half-dollar." With a disgusted snort, he dropped his hand faceup to reveal a hodgepodge of absolutely nothing. And only jack-high at that.

The dealer laughed and reached for the pot.

"Whoa, friend," Longarm cautioned. "Let's see your cards."

"I don't have to show them. Louie dropped out."

"No, Louie showed a jack-high hand. So how's about you show us that your hand beats that."

The dealer gave him a murderous look, but deposited his hand faceup for all to see. "There. Satisfied now?"

"I am, thank you." The silly bastard held nothing. Ace-high. The hand he laid down was an ace, a king, a ten, an eight, and one of Longarm's treys. Not only had he drawn to an inside straight, he'd done it with two cards missing. Incredible.

"Ante up, boys," the next man with the deal said.

"I'm out," Longarm told them.

"You mad about something, mister?"

Longarm forced a smile. "Not at all. I just want to take a break for a little while, that's all." He gathered up his change and dropped it into his pocket without bothering to count. He was a little light for the session, but nothing serious. And he certainly did not want to play any longer with men who had so little knowledge of and respect for the game. Longarm stubbed his cheroot out in a brass ashtray on the corner of the table, then walked over to the bar for a last drink before heading out along the creek in search of a soft spot to spread his bedroll.

He was about to order a shot of rye when the bartender's frowning expression caught his attention, and he looked in that direction.

A young man barely old enough to need to shave had just come in. The fellow was thin, with very pale blond hair and a scraggly mustache that looked like he'd best stay away from cats lest one lick the few hairs clean off his face. He wore a dark suit, an ancient Kossuth hat that was probably older than he was . . . and a brightly polished circle of steel on his coat lapel. The badge had a star scribed on it and colored in with black paint that was only a little bit chipped and flaking.

The bartender seemed not to like the youngster, who received no greetings from any of the patrons either. So, Longarm surmised, the local law came from the farming side of town.

The young man approached the bar, stopping two customers down from Longarm. "Everything all right tonight, Harry?"

The bartender turned his back on the youngster without giving the courtesy of a reply, and pretended to polish glasses.

The lawman—lawboy?—kept his composure and ignored the insult. But then, Longarm guessed, he was probably accustomed to this sort of thing.

He stood looking around at the now-silent saloon for several moments, then nodded his satisfaction that all seemed to be in order. With that he walked meekly out into the darkness.

Longarm turned back to the bar, where Harry the barman was once again on duty. With a broad smile but no comment on the obvious, Harry asked, "What would you like, friend?"

Chapter 13

Longarm woke with a stiff neck and a pain in his lower back. That sleeping out under the stars was romantic was a bunch of crap. A nice bed with a good mattress was a hell of a lot more comfortable. He pissed in the creek—upstream from the town, but what the hell, the sheep did it—but decided to forgo his morning shit until he got back to town and could use a proper outhouse. That was an awful lot more comfortable than braving Ma Nature's way too.

He swiftly broke his camp and rolled his gear, saddled the horse, and rode back to town to the café where he'd had supper the evening before.

"Good morning, sir." The woman was slim, tall, and wore her dark red hair pulled back in a severe bun. She had freckles. And a long, really quite elegant neck.

"Mornin', ma'am." Longarm removed his hat and bowed very slightly from the waist. "Where's small-stuff today?"

"If you mean my daughter, she is in school at this time of day, of course." She made it sound like Longarm was about as dumb as a post for not realizing where the child should be.

"I'd like some breakfast, ma'am. Whatever you have will be just fine. And coffee, o' course. If you don't mind, I'll step out back while you're getting it on the table." He dropped his hat on a chair at the corner table he'd chosen the previous evening, and went outside to find the back-house and washbasin. When he returned a few minutes later, there was coffee waiting for him and a plate full of griddle cakes.

"We don't have syrup," the woman told him, "but I could offer you some fruit compote if you wish."

"That'd be fine, ma'am."

She brought butter and several small crocks containing a variety of stewed fruits, peaches, and different kinds of berry. Longarm helped himself liberally to some of each. He was done with his meal and leaning back to enjoy a last cup of coffee when the young lawman came in.

The proprietress lifted her eyebrows in inquiry, but he shook his head no to the unspoken question about a meal and headed for Longarm's table.

Longarm had a better chance to look the young fellow over now. He could not say he was particularly impressed. The young man would do better to shave that undernourished excuse for a mustache. It only made him look like a boy trying too hard to look like a man.

Apart from that, the townie seemed ordinary enough. Longarm had only seen him from the side last night. Now he got a straight-on view and spotted the hard-edged bulge of a revolver butt worn in a shoulder rig beneath the suit coat. The badge was prominently displayed, but the gun was not. That suggested the boy was not letting himself get carried away with an exaggerated—and false—sense of authority the way some young deputies will.

"Mornin'," Longarm greeted, pushing a chair out by way of invitation. "Care for a cup of coffee?"

"Thank you." The fellow took the offered chair and dropped his battered old Kossuth onto the fourth chair at the table, Longarm's Stetson being on the other unoccupied seat.

Longarm motioned to the waitress for another cup of java.

"You're a stranger in our town," the fellow said.

"That's right, I am," Longarm agreed.

"Are you here on business or pleasure?"

"Business," Longarm said.

"And that business would be . . . ?"

"Mine," Longarm told him.

He had not intended to keep his job or his purpose here a secret. And still didn't really. It was the custom for federal officers to announce themselves to their local counterparts at the very least, and to cooperate with them whenever possible. But without consciously thinking about it beforehand, Longarm chose to remain silent on that subject for the time being.

The young man nodded. "All right. That's your privilege. I was only thinking to help."

"That's mighty kind of you. And you are . . . ?"

"Bill Thompson," the young man said. "Sheriff Thompson."

Longarm nodded. "Custis Long here."

Thompson offered his hand, and Longarm solemnly shook it.

The woman who ran the café brought Thompson's coffee. "Thank you, Maggie." He turned back to Longarm and smiled. "I see you had no difficulty finding the best eatery in our fair community, Mr. Long."

"Oh, go on with you now, Billy." She looked pleased, however. "You're as full of the blarney as ever your daddy was." She scurried off toward the kitchen. Longarm pushed the sugar bowl and can of condensed milk over to Thompson, who helped himself to both.

"Nice town," Longarm ventured.

"We like it."

"D'you have much in the way of trouble here?"

"Almost none."

"Lucky," Longarm said.

"They're good people here."

"On both sides of the river?"

"That's right," Thompson said. "On both sides." He stirred his coffee and took a small, experimental sip. Satisfied, he took a deeper swallow, then said, "Ever been here before?"

"No, this is my first trip."

"It didn't take you long to discover our . . . peculiarity."

"I noticed in the saloon last night that you aren't popular over on that side."

"Nobody can please everyone, Mr. Long. That's especially true of someone in my position."

"Is the sheriff here an elected position or an appointed one?"

"Are you thinking of running for office locally?" Thompson asked above the rim of the coffee cup.

"No. Just curious. Considerin' the way the two sides seem t' feel about one another."

"It is an elected position, Mr. Long."

"Have there always been more farmers than livestock growers?"

"Why do you assume there are?" He shrugged. "All right. You're correct. There are more on this side now. And in answer to the other part of that question, yes, it is a recent development." Thompson grinned, making him look even younger, almost impish. "We couldn't beat them at the polls before, but we could outbreed them. Now we can do both."

"Glory," Longarm said. "An honest politician."

"I'm no politician, Mr. Long. I'm the sheriff of a small county, trying to do my level best for everyone in this community."

"What about the town? Is there a town marshal in addition to you?"

"No, we aren't all that large nor all that prosperous. The Hart County sheriff handles any law enforcement needs inside the town as well as out. But like I already said, this is a quiet community. I can't complain about being overworked."

"No murders for you to solve or anything like that?"

"We haven't had a murder here since I was knee-high to a hound dog, Mr. Long. Is there something in particular you're trying to get at?"

"No. Sorry. I just get curious about things sometimes," Longarm said with a disarming smile.

Thompson finished his coffee and set the empty cup down. He stood. "If you will excuse me, Mr. Long, I'll be making my morning rounds now. My office is in the courthouse basement. Come see me if you need anything. Or if your curiosity starts acting up again."

"Thanks, Sheriff. I expect I'll do that by an' by."

"Any time, Mr. Long." Thompson retrieved his hat, nodded to Maggie, and left a nickel on the table before he left.

Longarm's impression was that he liked the young sheriff.

No murders in Weirville or Hart County since he was a kid. That was interesting too, wasn't it.

Longarm decided he would go get that shave now and eavesdrop on the barbershop chatter while he was at it.

Chapter 14

Longarm learned all manner of interesting things from listening in to conversations in the barbershop. For instance, a buyer for Deseret Fruit and Grain Company was due in town in another two weeks, and the dirt farmers were debating whether they should lock in a price for their produce this early or wait for the representative of Consolidated Produce, who wouldn't reach Weirville for another month, or trust that prices would rise again at harvest time. Whatever they did would be a gamble, and every year their financial lives depended on this sort of judgment months before they had a crop to sell.

He learned there was a fertilizer company that wanted their business badly enough to split the cost of haulage from the nearest railhead. What the farmers were debating was whether they could push the newcomer into a long-term contract to supply them when they hadn't yet gotten any experience with the quality of his fertilizers.

He also learned that, contrary to the impression the barber gave yesterday, there were a hell of a lot more farmers who came into the shop in the morning than there were sheepmen. Either that, or the sheepmen were unnaturally silent while they waited for the chair.

And he learned that a good barber—and this gent was a pretty good barber—requires damn little time to give a man a shave. For such a small town, the fellow did a right brisk business. It was Longarm's turn in the chair more quickly than he might have liked, eavesdropping on others' unprompted conversations being a sometimes excellent source of information.

"Good morning, sir. I see you decided against taking me up on that discount price," the barber told him.

"You weren't serious about that, were you?"

"Very serious. I charge fifteen cents for a regular shave, but only a dime after dinner."

"Then I'll have t' keep that in mind," Longarm said, not meaning it. Not, at least, until or unless he wanted a measure of privacy so he could speak with the barber.

By the time he got done with those few words his face was already moistened—there was no time for the application of a hot towel, darn it, and that was one of the great pleasures of an unhurried shave—and fully lathered. Harry took only a few seconds to slap his razor onto the hard leather strop before he began delicately scraping Longarm's whiskers off with a light, feathery touch of the blade.

"I had a visit from your sheriff this morning," Longarm ventured between strokes.

"You shouldn't ought to take that personal, friend," Harry said. "It's just that you're a stranger here and folks don't know yet where you fit in. Or if you fit in. If you see what I mean."

"Oh, I understand that, of course. No harm done and no offense taken. He said something, though, that I found curious. When I asked about how much crime there is hereabouts, Sheriff Thompson told me there hasn't been a murder around Weirville in years an' years."

"Now that you mention it, I suppose that'd be true." Harry paused a moment to think. Then he nodded. "Ayuh.

Ten, twelve years I'd say it's been." He raised his voice a little. "Ronnie. You've been here a long time. How long would you say it's been since Ed Borders was shot."

"What the hell are you bringing that up for, Harry?"

"Never mind why, just answer the question."

Ronnie had to give it some thought too. "Twelve years. I remember that because it was the year my first wife died while she was giving me my boy Dennis, and Denny will be twelve this June. So it was twelve years almost exactly."

"Did they figure out whoever did it?" Longarm asked.

"Huh! There wasn't any figuring had to be done. Everybody knew. Half the town saw it happen. Carl Wesler walked out of Happy Kyle's saloon and saw Ed sitting there with a wagon load of sweet potatoes. Carl was drunk, and even when he was sober he was mean. When he got to drinking he was hell in boots. He saw poor Ed sitting there minding his own business and just up and shot him right off that wagon."

"Did he hang for it?" Longarm asked.

Harry snorted. "Not on your life, mister. Not a Wesler. The others got together and sobered him up and made him leave this country quick before the sheriff was forced to do something about the murder. I mean, they couldn't have a sheepman . . . and a Wesler at that . . . hanged for shooting a fruit grower. So the sheriff dragged his feet, claiming he had to find the judge and get a warrant, long enough for the others to talk old Martha into sending her son away. Made her do it, the way I heard it. She didn't want to. She seemed to think like her boy did, that there wasn't anything all that wrong about shooting a fruit grower, so why should he run away. But the more sensible ones prevailed. They didn't want the feelings here to break out in open warfare, so they made her send Carl off so they could avoid a trial and . . ." Harry raised his voice again. "Ronnie."

"What is it now?"

"How long ago was it we heard Carl Wesler got killed?"

"Hell, I dunno. A year. Two maybe."

"Yeah, that sounds about right." Harry returned his attention to Longarm. "It turns out Carl didn't run very far. Down into New Mexico is all. I think that was a kind of open secret among the sheepmen, and probably he'd sneak home to visit his mama every now and then. Until he got himself drunk one too many times in a cantina in the Mexican quarter down in Taos. He picked a fight with some *campesino* and pulled a gun. Seemed there was half a dozen of that one's cousins standing behind Carl at the time, and he ended up with a bunch of knife wounds in his back. Stabbed him in his kidneys among other places. They say he lived long enough for the wounds to fester and died a terrible death. God's own punishment is the way a lot of folks here see it. Took a while, but judgment was passed." Harry used his towel to wipe away the remaining traces of lather, and removed the neck cloth from Longarm's lap. "There you go, friend. You look bright as a new penny."

Longarm thanked him and paid for his shave.

A dozen years since last there was any violence around here, he was thinking as he left the barbershop. And both parties to that murder were dead and buried now.

So much for that line of thinking.

He untied his horse from the public rail and swung onto the saddle. There was a livery on the sheep side of the creek that looked like it was well tended and should be reliable. He wanted to buy some grain for the animal. Overnight grazing was good, but grain was better.

Not that he expected to have to use the horse hard now

that he was here. But a man should always take the best possible care of his mount, and this was too good a horse to let it lose flesh.

He put the animal into a trot, pondering his next line of questioning while he rode.

Chapter 15

Longarm had to consult the scraps of information Billy Vail gave him back in Denver so he could get the name of the county commissioner who'd demanded this investigation. If anybody wanted to call it that. Damned waste of time was what it really was. But then the government was the one handing out pay; the government, therefore, was the one that got to call the shots.

Adam Terhune. That was the name of the fellow whose goodwill the governor wanted. Longarm supposed he would have to show the colors if he expected to make this Terhune any sort of happy.

Of course if he *really* wanted to please Terhune, there would be an easy way to do that. Just find out which side of the creek the man represented, then arrest somebody from the other side. Almost anybody would do.

That did seem a mite much, he decided. But at the very least, he could talk to Terhune and let him know that his complaints were being taken seriously back in the state capital.

An inquiry at the livery, where he bought a gallon of mixed oats and wheat, told him where he could find the commissioner.

"Adam's place is yonder," the hostler said, pointing. "See that blue-slate roof? You can barely see it peeping over top of Silas Bannerman's house there. That's right, over there. That's where Adam lives."

"Would he likely be there during the day?" Longarm asked.

"Generally is. Walks over to the courthouse about mid-morning generally to see what's up in the clerk's office and like that, then goes home for lunch and a nap after. You're already too late to catch him at Hilda's place."

"Hilda's?"

"That's the café just the far side of the courthouse. Adam and some of the other boys take their coffee there of a morning. It's where everybody knows they can catch up with them if they want to discuss county business. But he'd be gone from there by now probably."

"Mind if I ask what Commissioner Terhune does?"

"Sheepman, o' course. Been here a long time, Adam has. One of the original settlers in Hart County."

"But he lives in town," Longarm observed.

"Hell, most of them do. The big producers, that is. They got Mexicans an' Basques to go out and live with the woolies. The owners don't have to. Not now that they've got some money in their pockets. Was different in the early days, but now they've got settled and respectable."

Longarm smiled. "Friend, you've been a big help. Thanks. Tell you what. Since I won't have to be riding out anyplace, how about I leave my horse here for the day. I'll pick him up sometime this evening."

"That's fine. Day only . . . he'll have meadow hay and clean water . . . that'll be a dime. Nickel more if you want him grained."

"I'll take the graining, and I thank you." Longarm touched the brim of his Stetson and headed for the house with the blue-slate roof.

• • •

The commissioner's house had an air of comfortable prosperity about it. So did the commissioner.

Terhune answered the door himself. He was in shirt sleeves and house slippers, but his boiled shirt was crisply starched and his tie was snug at his collar. He stood about five foot ten or so, and probably weighed upward of three hundred pounds, not all of which was fat. He looked like he might have been a handful thirty years ago. "What can I do for you, sir?" he asked with a smile and an offered handshake.

"I need a little of your time if I may, sir. In private."

Terhune acted like he received that sort of request every day. And for all Longarm knew, perhaps he did. "Very well, young man. Come inside." There was no hesitation whatsoever.

Terhune led Longarm to an oak-paneled study dominated by a massive fireplace on one side and a huge roll-top desk on the other. It would have taken several span of oxen and a helluva stout wagon to ship that desk in. Leather upholstered wing-back chairs flanked a small game table in front of the fireplace. Terhune motioned Longarm to one of those and sat in the other himself.

"Regina," he said without raising his voice.

A side door opened and a tiny woman of indeterminate age and ancestry stood there.

"Coffee, sir?" Terhune asked Longarm.

"Please."

"Two coffees, Regina."

The woman bobbed her head and withdrew without speaking.

"Now, sir. May I inquire as to your business?"

Chapter 16

"Well, now. I have to say I'm surprised. And pleased. A United States marshal. Imagine that. I never expected this."

"You'll keep this strictly quiet, I hope," Longarm repeated for the third or fourth time.

"Absolutely, my boy. My lips are sealed."

"The governor is naturally concerned about the things you've told him, and he discussed it at length with the U.S. Attorney for the district. They thought it best to send a federal officer." That was a bunch of booshwah, but what the hell. It was what was called for here . . . in the absence of any crime or criminals. This whole trip was about mending somebody else's political fences, but if Billy Vail said it needed doing, then Custis Long would damn well do it. And butter up this pissant county commissioner until the man was so greasy he couldn't walk uphill.

"I am pleased, Deputy Long. I must admit that I am very pleased."

"That's good, sir. But please call me Longarm. All my friends do."

Terhune beamed, reminding Longarm anew that it is

nigh impossible to overdo things when flattering a politician.

"Now if you could tell me some of the particulars of your concern, sir, I would appreciate it. About all I know at this point is that some citizens of this county have died, and you believe they were the victims of foul play. I'm also given to understand, sir, that the local, um, authorities have declined to investigate."

"Declined. Now that's putting a pretty face on incompetence, Dep . . . Longarm, my friend."

"Incompetence is a strong word, sir."

"All right. I shall use another. Partisanship. Is that one better?"

"This has something to do with the, uh, differences between the sheepmen and the farmers here?"

"This has everything to do with that, friend Longarm," Terhune responded. "Those people will not listen to sweet reason. Now that is the long and the short of it. Five prominent citizens of this county have mysteriously died over the past two years, Longarm. Five good men. Five men who pioneered this county. Men who came in here when this land supported nothing but sagebrush and jackrabbits and made something of it. I know how hard it was for them, Longarm, because I was one of them. We came in here with nothing but grit and determination and we built something fine. Now those farmers and fruit growers want to take it all away from us. They want to profit from what we have built, and they aren't satisfied with their fair share of the land's bounty here. They want to deny us the use of what is ours, and they want to force us off our own land."

Longarm raised an eyebrow.

Terhune waved the inquiry away as if of no importance. "I don't mean literally. They aren't resorting to overt action toward that end. But make no mistake, sir, that *is* the end they have in mind. No, what they have been doing is trying to worm their way into public office. They want to enact laws . . . landhold taxes, for instance . . . that will make it impossible for us to continue on this land that we carved from the wilderness and made safe for the likes of them."

Now that, Longarm knew, was a whopper of major proportion. Made safe? The implication naturally was that things had somehow been dangerous before the sheepmen arrived to tame the land and drive out the savages. Except to the best of Longarm's knowledge, there never had been any danger from Indians in or close to what was now Hart County.

The Utes stayed mostly well to the south, where the hunting was good and water plentiful. The Snakes and Arapaho had lived nowhere near. Even the lowly Diggers seldom came this far east.

As far as Longarm knew, the biggest danger a pioneer in this area would've faced would have been sunburn or maybe snakebite.

But then it sounded ever so much better the way Commissioner Terhune told the story.

"Now, after five murders, that fruit-loving sheriff of theirs . . . and what a farce that election was, let me tell you . . . now that young smart-aleck won't even look into the deaths. The boy should be removed from office for malfeasance, Longarm. And would have been before now if the farmers hadn't packed the county commission with their own."

Longarm's eyebrow headed for the ceiling again.

"The fruit growers hold three seats now. We used to be in the majority, but now we sheepmen have been reduced to two. And we are keeping those only because of the district boundaries. God help us if the farmers ever decide to ramrod through a gerrymandered redistricting. We will become outcasts on our own land, I tell you."

"Yes, sir. About these, uh, deaths . . . ?"

"Oh. Yes. The murders. Like I said, there have been five of them." Terhune shook his head and took a swallow of the coffee his maid had delivered.

Despite the early hour, Longarm thought he could detect a whiff of something other than coffee in that cup. Could be the commissioner had himself a bit of a drinking problem. Longarm's own cup, he was sorry to say, held nothing but coffee.

"Naturally no one paid any mind to the first death. After all, people do die. It's nature's way, and as far as I can tell, there is no getting around it. We all have to go sometime. But these men were taken in their prime, sir, every one of them. First Mason Boatwright. Then John Evans. Jace Wilcox. Lee McElroy. And finally Benson Evans, John's younger brother. Every one of them taken in the span of less than two years. Since, I might add, that damnable upstart Thompson became sheriff and the road was clear for them to begin killing us without having to fear interference from what is laughably called law here these days."

"You say the deaths began occurring shortly after Sheriff Thompson took office?"

"That's right. Mason died . . . I think it was about two, perhaps three weeks after the election."

"And how did these people die. Commissioner?"

"Came down sick with a flux of some sort. No one thought anything sinister about it to begin with, of course. Mason had been in the pink of good health, but people do get sick."

"Did a doctor look at him?"

"We don't have a regular doctor. Just Harry Sprague. He's our barber. But he's good at stanching wounds and sewing up cuts and the like. He can apply a poultice or dose a fellow with ipecac, that sort of thing. But he isn't a regular doctor."

"What about a coroner? Do you have a doctor come in for coroner's inquests?"

"No, we don't have a coroner. Haven't had a coroner's inquest in . . . I can't even remember if we even had one the time young Wesler shot that farmer." Terhune frowned and took another swallow of his coffee. "You know, Longarm, now that I think on it, I can't recall if we've ever had an actual coroner's inquest here. Damned if I know what we'd do if we needed one. Call Harry to testify, I suppose, and let a jury hear it out. Sort of like a grand jury except we'd call it an inquest instead."

"So no one well versed in the practice of medicine ever saw Boatwright. How about the others who died?"

Terhune shrugged. "Same thing with them, pretty much. They were fine and dandy. Then they got sick. Next thing anybody knew they were dead."

"And you think all five are connected," Longarm said.

"I know they were. And don't ask me what evidence I have. Young Thompson keeps yapping at me about evidence. What I have is a gut feeling, Longarm. I just plain know those friends of mine were all murdered. I don't know how. I don't even know why. But I know damn good and well they were murdered."

"Has anyone else died in Hart County during the last two years?"

"Of course. Ted and Thelma Bates lost two youngsters to a flux this past winter. The Bateses are farmers, you understand, but not bad people. I went to the funeral for those children and I meant every word of sympathy that I told them. And, let me see, fall before last Eric Conway got kicked in the head by a horse. He lingered more than a week before he was taken. None of those deaths was murder, of course. The five others are."

"Yes, sir."

"Will you be investigating the murders then, Longarm?"

"Yes, sir, I will. That's what they sent me here for."

"Good. I'm glad to hear it."

"Mind you now, I can't do anything until or unless I find some evidence to support a charge of murder. But I can promise you that I will look."

"I can't ask fairer than that, Longarm. Thank you."

"You can thank the governor, sir, and the U.S. Attorney."

"I'm in their debt," Terhune said.

Which, Longarm realized, was the entire purpose of him being here. Now Terhune owed the governor. Someday, in some way, that obligation would be called in.

It seemed a hell of a way to go about enforcing the law, Longarm thought. But then when you live in the real world, there are real inconveniences that go along with the good.

He stood and offered his hand to the Hart County commissioner. "Please keep my identity secret at least for the time being, sir. I want to be able to move freely on the other side of the creek while I begin this investigation."

Besides, he respectfully declined to say, by remaining anonymous he could avoid the embarrassment of being known as that federal idiot who was conducting a murder investigation into deaths by natural causes.

Terhune accompanied him to the door, where Regina met them with Longarm's hat. "Good-bye, sir," said Longarm, "I'll report back to you when I know something."

"I look forward to that, friend Longarm."

Four days, Longarm thought as he made his way back toward the nearest bridge over to the farmers' side of town. Four days ought to be enough to satisfy the governor—nothing short of an arrest would really satisfy Terhune, he believed, but four days ought to be enough to convince him that a sincere effort had been made—and then Longarm could go the hell home.

In the meantime, he could enjoy fruit pie and cobbler on one side of town, and rye whisky and poker on the other. Fair and unbiased always.

He took out a cheroot and lighted it, feeling very much at peace with the world now that his real mission had been accomplished and the governor's marker placed.

Chapter 17

Longarm changed his mind about staying in town the whole day. After all, what the hell could he do for all that time without people commenting and the word quite possibly getting back to Commissioner Terhune? If Longarm spent the next few days playing the role of a feckless layabout, it was sure to be noticed. And after all, Terhune knew him as a cold-eyed hunter of . . . a nameless flux. Or something.

In any event, Longarm was concerned that public idleness might destroy the impression the governor and Billy Vail wanted him to leave with the now-obligated county commissioner. So he needed to give the appearance of being busy with this investigation that did not in fact exist.

That would be easier done, he decided, if he was not right there under the watchfully suspicious eyes of the entire population of Weirville.

Strangers stand out in any small community, but here, with half the people's already established mistrust of the half from the other side of the creek, that normal level of suspicion would surely be magnified.

Longarm lighted a cheroot and strode rapidly to the livery stable where he'd left his horse. The animal's coat gleamed from a fresh brushing. Nearly all the lingering remnants of its shaggy winter coat had been curried away, and when Longarm walked in it was in the process of seeking out the last few oat grains in a bucket before tackling the hay bunk. The horse had been mighty well cared for in Longarm's absence. And hours in advance of the time the hostler expected Longarm's return too. None of this was for show; it was the work of a man who cared about horses and went to the trouble of doing his job almighty well. Longarm was impressed.

He sought out the livery man and told him so. The man only shrugged. But Longarm could see that the compliment pleased him.

Longarm took his gear down off the rack beside the tack room door and saddled the horse, then handed the hostler a half-dollar.

"Just a second, mister, while I get your change outa my seegar box in there."

"No change," Longarm told him.

"It's only fifteen cents you owe me."

"I remember."

"Thank you, mister. Thank you a lot."

Longarm only shrugged. He mounted the bay and headed for open country.

Man's stubborn industriousness was a source of wonder sometimes, Longarm thought as he sat atop the bay horse with a cheroot between his teeth and contemplated the ongoing work that lay across the creek from him.

A ditch was being dug here. One helluva ditch actually. It was a good six feet wide and four deep, and stretched straight as a bow string for a good half mile away to the south before he lost sight of it.

Irrigation. That would be the purpose of it whenever it was completed. For now it stopped about two rods short of the creek. Presumably the final cut wouldn't be made and the gates built until the downstream end of the irrigation system was dug and ready. Lumber for the gates was stacked on the creek bank ready for use, as was a small keg that he guessed held hardware.

Longarm found it interesting that no one found it necessary to guard either the ditch or the construction supplies.

It looked like the sheepmen and the dirt farmers didn't care for each other, but had no thought of taking extreme measures against their neighbors either. This was a range war—if you could call it that—that was being fought strictly at the ballot box.

Longarm had to like that. It made a peace officer's job much more pleasant if there was actual peace, peace being a commodity far easier to keep than to create.

He finished his cheroot and flicked the stub into an eddy of shallow water at the edge of the creek, then turned the bay's head and took it down into the creek.

The water in midstream barely reached his boots. Deep enough to wet the soles, but not so deep as to submerge his spurs. The creek here was not much wider than the ditch that was being built on the bank in front of him.

His horse climbed out onto the bank and shook itself doglike even though its legs and belly were the only things that got wet. Longarm patiently waited for it to get that out of its system, then rode south along the raw, dark cut in the earth.

Now that the ground was exposed to view, he could see why a farmer or fruit grower would be interested in this land. The soil looked good. A little rocky, but nothing a man with patience and a plow couldn't cope with. More to the point, it was not the pale clay or sand that is found underlying much better-watered grassland than this. Hart County might not get a lot of rainfall—and did not, as its scanty foliage would attest—but the soil beneath that scrubby growth was a middlin' shade of brown that was just short of being loamy.

It was not something Longarm liked either to admit or remember, but as a boy he'd had more experience than he ever wanted holding the handles of a moldboard plow and staring at a mule's ass. He knew a little about soil, and this looked much richer and more useful than he would have suspected.

The only thing holding farming back here was water.

And it looked like the farmers intended to take care of that with this irrigation project.

It occurred to Longarm that a project like this would require a helluva lot of labor. Not much in the way of materials, of course. A single scraper and team could do the job given time enough to do it. A cooperative effort by a bunch of participants would get it done sooner. And a public works project using county tax money to hire construction crews could get it done in practically no time at all.

If there were any murders here . . . if, say, sheepmen were being killed . . . a possible motive could be a desire among some farmers to get rid of those sheepmen who were politically powerful in order that the farmers could pack the county commission with their own candidates and appropriate tax money for the swift completion of this irrigation ditching system.

But that was if there were any murders taking place here.

Which of course there were not.

Longarm's chin lifted and he rose off the saddle to peer ahead. He could hear the yip of barking dogs, and he thought, but wasn't quite sure, he could hear as well the thin sound of a human voice.

Somebody in trouble?

Wouldn't hurt to go take a look, he thought.

He settled onto the seat of his saddle again and bumped the horse into a lope.

Chapter 18

"Lady, stop it. Lady! Quit!"

The woman looked terrified. The pups looked like they were having the time of their young lives.

Of course the pups were having fun. As far as they were concerned, this was nothing but a game. They were playing. It was the woman who was taking it seriously.

The woman sat—sat, stood, turned, jumped, swiveled, cowered—on the seat of a ratty-looking buckboard that had one wheel buried hub-deep in a mud hole where she'd been trying to cross the incomplete ditch.

The brown and black pups, five of them, were jumping and yipping and tear-assing around in joyful circles, making the woman's horses rear and making the woman bawl and curse and slap at them ineffectually with the lash of her buggy whip.

"Lady. Calm down now. Please."

"Oh, thank God. Do something. You have a gun. Shoot them."

A black pup with a blaze of white on its chest took advantage of her momentary inattention to jump high and capture the popper at the end of her whip. The dog's weight yanked the object out of the woman's hand, and the pup took off at a mad dash to show off its prize. The others gave chase, and soon all five of them were scrambling for possession of the tasty leather treasure.

Longarm managed to keep from laughing. But barely.

Of course to the woman, the whole thing was a tragedy barely averted. Damn critters were trying to kill and eat her. Or so she appeared to be convinced.

"Shoot them. Shoot them."

Longarm grinned. "How's about I get your whip back instead. Can you settle for that?" He stepped off his horse and took a wrap with the rein ends on one of the back wheels of her wagon.

"Oh, sir. Be careful. They'll turn on you as soon as they've destroyed my whip."

"I'll try an' be real careful, ma'am, thank you."

He clapped his hands loudly to get the pups' attention, and five heads came up, ears pricked and tongues lolling. "C'mere, you little heathens. D'you know you've scared the lady? You ought t' be ashamed," he told them in a voice filled with submerged laughter that the pups could surely hear even if the woman did not. "Come here now. Come on." He clapped his hands again and bent down, and the mob of pups came racing to him, yipping with renewed excitement.

Longarm bent down.

The woman screamed.

The fastest pup launched itself into the air toward Longarm's throat. With a chuckle he cradled it in his arms, and let it cover his neck and cheeks with wet doggy "kisses" while the other four squirmed and wriggled around his boots like a pack of hairy worms.

Laughing openly now, Longarm carried the happy, boisterous puppy to the side of the wagon so the woman could see just how much danger she'd been in. "They were just bein' playful, miss. They're hardly more than babies. Just having a romp, that's all. Only way they could hurt you would be to lick you half t' pieces."

"I . . . I'm afraid of dogs," she said, that information not exactly startling under the circumstances.

"Yes, ma'am, but they're too young t' understand that." He dropped the puppy he'd been holding and picked up another. That one quivered with excitement and dribbled a little pee onto his shirt while its tongue went for his ears. "Hey! That tickles." He laughed and turned the pup to hold it in the crook of one arm while he scratched its belly with his free hand. "These are sheep dogs, miss. There isn't a mean bone in them. Not unless you're a coyote or some such varmint trying t' harm one o' their sheep. An' even then they'd rather scare you off than bite you."

"They would have no trouble frightening me away, believe me."

"Yes, ma'am. You want t' pet this one for a second?"

"No, of course not. I . . . wait." Tentatively, prepared to snatch a bloody stump back at a moment's notice, she reached out and lightly brushed the ear of the pup Longarm was holding.

The happy animal turned too quickly for her to avoid and licked her hand. She shivered and drew back. But Longarm thought that for half a moment there she'd liked it. That was enough, though. He did not want to push his luck. He set the young dog down and let it go scampering away to show off to its litter mates. Longarm retrieved the slightly chewed and decidedly wet buggy whip and returned it to its owner.

"Go on now," he called to the pups. "Go home."

As if they knew what he was saying—and hell, they were sheep dogs, so maybe they did at that—the pups began gamboling and barking and racing off toward the distant creek.

"Children," Longarm said. "They're just exactly like children, that's all."

"Thank you for rescuing me, sir."

"You weren't ever in any danger."

"I'm not so sure about that. If you hadn't come along when you did . . ." She shuddered, her fears returning now that the pups' good nature was no longer on active display.

"Yes, well, tell you what. Let's see if we can't get you unstuck from this mess."

It would mean a cleaning job on his boots, and a clean shirt too, but there wasn't any help for it. Somebody was going to have to lift that wheel so the horses could pull out of the bog, and Longarm couldn't see any other candidates lining up for the privilege.

"If you got that whip handy, ma'am, I'll want you t' spank the team on soon as I give you the word, okay? On three now. One . . . two . . . ungh!"

Chapter 19

At her insistence, Longarm followed the woman home, a jog of less than half a mile that ended at a small cabin set on a bare but promising patch of flat ground. There was a corral and shed for the horses, and another shed for implements, plus the outhouse. A pump housing protruded from the ground midway between the cabin door and the watering trough in the corral.

A garden plot or very small truck garden—Longarm could not be sure which as it was overlarge for a household garden, but too small to produce much income if that was its purpose—lay on the side of the cabin opposite the corral, and behind the house there was an area that was dotted with sticks stuck upright in the ground. Except on closer inspection, the sticks turned out to be very small, very bare saplings of some sort. Apparently the planting here had only recently begun, but eventually would result in an orchard of fairly considerable scope. He had no idea what fruit was being grown.

Longarm helped the woman down and said, "I'll see t' the horses, ma'am. You go on inside and relax. You sure you want me t' stop in? Your husband might not appreciate a stranger inside the house."

"I'm sure. And please. Put your horse in the pen too. This will take a while."

"This." He had no idea what "this" was supposed to be. Obviously she had something in mind, though.

"Yes'm." He stripped the harness from her horses and put them in the corral, then hung the harness inside the shed, not at all sure about which pegs were intended for what, but doing the best he could. He also, as courtesy required in light of her comment, pulled his saddle and hung that on the top fence rail before putting his saddle horse into the corral with the pair of cobs.

He stopped at the pump for a quick washup. It did nothing to get his boots and shirt clean, but it was the best he could do. Then he collected his coat and vest from the back of his saddle—it was still damned cold without them, but he hadn't wanted to get them muddy—and went to tap on the door.

"Come in."

He let himself in to find himself surrounded by the homey scents of baking bread and . . . something else too, although he could not call to mind just what the other was.

"Would you mind filling the bucket, please? I need more water to wash with."

"Of course." For a few seconds, though, he stood looking at the woman, who was busy doing something at a sideboard, standing with her back to him.

Now that she had shed her long coat and all-encompassing hat, she was not a bad-looking figure of a woman. She was of medium height and very slim, with a tiny waist and narrow hips. She had a long and quite elegant neck, and fiery red hair worn in a tight bun at the nape of her neck. He guessed she would be somewhere in her late twenties or very early thirties.

"I won't be but a moment," he said. He took the bucket that had been placed beside the door and filled it at the pump, then returned. "Where d'you want this, ma'am?"

"Over here by the range, please. Pour it into the reservoir. And would you mind bringing in another?"

"Not at all." He poured that bucketful into the hot-water reservoir built onto the side of the oven, then carried in three more, the first two of those also going into the reservoir until it was quite full, and the third set on the floor ready for whatever use she had for it.

"Thank you very much, sir."

"You're welcome, ma'am."

"Would it be too personal a question, sir, if I were to ask your name?"

"I haven't . . . ? No, I reckon I haven't at that. Sorry." He quickly corrected that oversight. "And you are . . . ?"

"Sissy Beckham. And before you ask, that is my real name and not a nickname. God knows why. I haven't any brothers or sisters to hold responsible for it, and my mother died before I was old enough to ask her why she would give me such an awful name. But it is mine and I am not ashamed of it. Also, Mr. Long, I see you looking around my home. If you are wondering why there are no signs of a Mr. Beckham, it is because no such animal exists. I am a single woman, and I am here because I want to make a future for myself that does not involve being a housemaid in someone else's house or engaging in the only other employment opportunity that is open to women. I am sure you know what I mean by that."

"Yes, ma'am . . . uh, miss. Reckon I do at that."

"Now, sir. Having assured you that I am not a woman of ill repute, I have a question for you. Would you please take your clothes off?"

Longarm's expression must have reflected his surprise, because Sissy Beckham burst into laughter.

"I am sorry, Mr. Long. Well, a little bit sorry. But I couldn't help myself. I wanted to see what you would do, and you did not disappoint me."

"Whew. Glad we got that cleared up. Kinda."

"I really do want your shirt, though. It needs washing. And I want to clean those boots too. Oh, dear. Look. The mud was deeper than I thought. You've gotten your trousers muddy too. I shouldn't wash them, but I can sponge them off enough that tomorrow you will be able to brush the last bits away and not see a thing."

While she talked, she was busy rummaging in a rather nice-looking cedar chest that sat at the foot of her bed. She pulled out a sheet, examined and quickly rejected it, then settled on a very large linen tablecloth that had an oak-leaf pattern embroidered along the border. She handed the tablecloth to him.

"Take your clothes off, please, and wrap this around you like a toga. It will make you ever so distinguished-looking. Julius Caesar with a six-shooter." She laughed. "If I scare you, you can belt the gun on over your toga."

"I dunno, miss. I might have t' do that. Educated women are scary t' be sure."

"Suit yourself. Just give me your shirt and trousers."

He glanced down at the mess that wagon wheel had made of his shirt, and decided it probably was a good idea to comply with the request. Miss Beckham turned her back while he put his coat and hat aside and kicked out of his boots, then placed his gunbelt onto a small table beside her rocking chair and shucked out of his britches and shirt.

He was standing there in smallclothes and socks when he caught her peeping at him.

"That wasn't an accident," he accused.

She only laughed. And boldly turned to face him, an impish expression on her face. That face was, he decided, not beautiful. But it was damn sure interesting. Bright eyes. Thin nose. Thin lips. And that long, long neck.

Longarm wrapped the tablecloth around himself.

Wrapped his dignity around himself too, such as he still had.

Sissy collected his clothing and said, "Sit down and relax. The water will be hot in a minute. I'm afraid I haven't any coffee to offer, but I brew a mean cup of tea."

"That'd be fine, thanks." Tea was not his favorite beverage, but he could drink it when need be and not gag on it.

He sat in the rocker, picked up a thick, chunky book that was lying on the table beside his Colt, and opened it to the marker. *The Collected Works of Shakespeare (Abridged)*, She was in the middle of *Othello* at the moment. The book, he saw, had seen a lot of use.

He got another surprise when she brought his tea. She'd laced it already with canned milk and a goodly amount of sugar . . . and with something else as well.

"Do you like it?"

"Very much. What is it?"

"Apple brandy. I've always thought it goes especially well with tea." She smiled and returned to the tub, where she was pummeling and twisting his no-longer-muddy shirt. It was going to take a while for that shirt to dry out now, he reflected.

Not that he was in any hurry to be going. The cabin was warm, the fortified tea was downright pleasant. And so was the company. Damned if this woman wasn't interesting, never mind that she was a trifle odd.

Truth was, he liked her.

Longarm took up the book again and opened it to *Hamlet*. Much more interesting yarn, he'd always thought, than *Othello*.

Chapter 20

"There," she said finally. "Your shirt should be dry in an hour or two if the breeze keeps up, and your trousers will dry almost as soon. I didn't give them a complete washing, but I think they will be clean enough. The boots, I'm afraid, I can't do anything more for. You will have to get those freshly blacked in town."

"That's fine, miss."

"I'll make some lunch for you in a few minutes, but first I need to wash you off."

"No need for you t' do that, miss."

"Oh, but of course there is. That puppy licked you. That can't be at all clean. Besides, it peed on you. I know good and well that came through your shirt, and I couldn't abide the thought of that staying on your skin. Stand up now."

Longarm laid the book aside and stood.

"Here. You can knot this around your waist if you insist on being modest," she said, sliding the tablecloth toga off his shoulders. She stood for a moment looking at his chest, her expression unreadable. Then she turned and fetched a basin of warm water and a small piece of sacking.

She scrubbed his face and neck first, then proceeded down onto his body, stomach first, where the pup might possibly have peed, but also higher, where it most certainly could not have.

Before long, he had to notice, the pace of her washing became slower and her touch more a series of lingering caresses.

If there'd been any doubt at all—and there hadn't been much to begin with—she dispelled it when she tugged the tablecloth free at his waist and let it fall, leaving him standing in nothing but drawers, socks, and a hard-on.

"Oh, my!" But the comment had to do not with shock, but with amazement.

She set her basin and washcloth aside and knelt, drawing the socks down and pulling them off his feet.

Then she did the same thing with his shorts. Longarm stood naked before her.

With a smile Sissy retrieved her washbasin and began gently but very carefully washing Longarm's cock.

She was, he decided, a very fastidious lady.

Not that he was complaining.

Sissy Beckham had a redhead's typical skin, very pale and so thin he could see the blue tracery of blood vessels close to the surface, especially on the firm little disks that were her tits. They were no bigger than inverted saucers. But they, and the tiny, pale pink nipples that perched atop them, were unusually sensitive. When Longarm licked and suckled them, Sissy began to moan and writhe beneath him. A few moments more and she had a gasping, shuddering climax. And he hadn't yet gotten around to so much as touching her pussy.

"Quick on the trigger," he observed.

"Lucky me," she agreed with a low chuckle.

"An' me as well," he said. He took his time, kissing her thoroughly and enjoying the feel of her tongue probing his mouth. Then he bent to her nipple again, and once more was able to produce that same result after a minute or two of licking.

She cried out loudly when she climaxed, and clutched hard at the hair on the back of his head. Almost immediately she apologized. "Did I hurt you?"

"Not yet." He kissed her again. "But how are you gonna act when I put it inside you?"

"I don't know. Oh, my. Do you think it could be dangerous? Perhaps you should stand over there when you do it so I won't be able to reach you."

He looked at her, and Sissy began to laugh.

He smiled. "I like a girl that knows how t' have fun in bed."

"But it is fun, you know. It is ever so much fun."

"Reckon I'd have t' agree with you, ma'am," he said in a mock-solemn tone.

Sissy laughed again. And reached down to grab his cock and tug him over her.

Her thighs were already spread wide, eager to receive him, and her pussy was dripping wet and just as receptive. Longarm poised above her for a moment and Sissy guided him into her sheath.

He let himself down slowly, giving her body time to accommodate the length and the thickness of his shaft. He felt the heat of her body welcome him, surrounding and clasping his flesh.

It was rather obvious that Sissy Beckham was no virgin. But she was almost as tight as one. He groaned aloud at the feel of her body beneath his, and she wrapped herself around him from one end to the other, enveloping him with her arms, pussy, and legs all at the same time. Not content with that, she craned her neck to reach his ear and pulled that into her mouth so she could hold him inside herself there too.

Longarm began to thrust, slowly at first and then with

greater speed and intensity, his belly slapping hard against hers as he pumped and hammered at her slender body.

It had always been his experience that appearances to the contrary, it just isn't possible for a man to break a woman in two with nothing but a pecker for a weapon. But that never kept him from trying.

Longarm felt his sap begin to gather almost immediately, and Sissy, her pump already primed by two climaxes, convulsed in throes of intense pleasure within seconds. She clutched at him with all her strength and screamed loudly—right into his ear, unfortunately—as she came.

Longarm was only seconds behind her in reaching his first explosion. He plunged into her as if determined to throw his whole body into her hot cavity, and his juices splashed deep inside her.

He was gasping when finally he disengaged from her and rolled onto his back at her side.

"Wow!" he whispered.

"Give me a minute to rest. Then I'll get you ready again. Have you ever had a woman take you in her mouth?" she asked.

"In her mouth? No, I don't expect anybody's ever done that t' me before," he lied without expression.

"Then you're in for a treat," she told him. She smiled and started at the top, kissing him first, then licking his throat and nipples, pausing there to suckle briefly, before running her tongue over his belly and down to the hard-on that Longarm was already displaying.

Sissy was right, he decided shortly. It was a treat. And the skinny redhead was certainly able to dispel any ugly claims that women with thin lips can't give great blow jobs.

Chapter 21

It was late in the afternoon by the time Longarm's clothes were dry. Or at least that was the excuse he was using to remain in the lusty redhead's bed, not that it took so very much urging to keep him there. Eventually, though, they both ran out of energy, and he figured he ought to head back to his creek-side camp so he would have time to put everything in order before darkness turned an easy task into an annoyance.

He leaned down from the saddle to kiss her good-bye, and with a grin said, "If you ever decide t' give up farming, lady, you could make a fortune in that other line o' work."

"I think that was supposed to be a compliment," she said with a laugh.

Longarm kissed her again and bumped the bay horse into motion.

He cut across country rather than follow the irrigation ditch, and reached the creek about a mile above Weirville. The horse splashed across to the other side, and Longarm found the same spot he'd used the night before. It had been comfortable enough, and he already had a fire ring there. He unsaddled the bay and spread his bedroll before pulling together the makings for a small fire.

Sissy had fed him in addition to draining his juices, so he was not really very hungry. But a pot of coffee sounded mighty good. He dipped water from the creek and put that over the flames to boil along with a handful of ready-ground coffee—more expensive than buying roasted beans and cracking them yourself, but a helluva lot more convenient when on the trail—and prepared to settle down for the night.

His coffee wasn't yet stout enough to drink when he saw a horseman approaching from the direction of town. Somebody following the creek and passing by, Longarm thought. He nodded a polite hello to the fellow when he came near, then knelt beside his fire to check on the progress of the coffee. It was commencing to smell mighty good, the way only coffee boiled over an open fire really can.

Behind him he heard the horse come to a stop. It stamped and blew, but the rider said nothing.

Expecting an invitation to have a cup of the good stuff, Longarm figured. And what the hell. He stood, the cartilage in his knees cracking, and turned. "Howdy."

"You're Long." It was a statement, not a question. And this quite obviously was no bummer looking for a cup of java.

"Do I know you?" Longarm asked.

"No, but you prob'ly heard o' me. Name's Jedediah Jerome Gable."

"I've heard the name before," Longarm said. And so he had. He'd never met Gable nor seen any flyers on the man, but he had the reputation of a killer. "I thought you were down in Arizona Territory."

"Last month. You heard about that, did you?"

"Obviously." What he'd heard was that Gable gunned down two men outside the town of Darby.

"It was a fair fight. Did you hear that too?"

"What I heard was that you goaded those men into a fight they couldn't possibly win, then shot them to pieces when you didn't have to." He had also heard that Gable was working for a sheep outfit at the time, hogging range from interlopers who wanted to homestead and take water rights for their farms.

And wasn't that interesting, he thought now. And if Gable was in Arizona killing farmers for one sheepman just a month back, what was he doing here now? And how long had he been here?

Looked like there could be a range war in the making, although it probably had not a damn thing to do with the deaths by natural causes that had brought Longarm here.

Jedediah Gable did not look very happy with Longarm's comment, which as much as accused him of murder regardless of how a coroner's jury might have ruled it afterward. "You're a cheeky son of a bitch, ain't you?"

"I'm cheeky," Longarm agreed, "but you'd best put a bridle on your tongue or it's gonna get you in trouble."

"Not from the likes of you, it won't," Gable declared.

The man was big enough, Longarm saw, and built for speed and power, not just bull muscle. He wore a pair of ivory-handled revolvers that hung low on his thighs and were tied down there.

A rig like that was undoubtedly impressive as hell . . . to anyone who knew little about gunpowder that was burned with serious intent.

Fact was, hanging a gun that low made it quick to grab, but slower to cock and get into action than a higher carry.

What was really stupid was that being tied in line with the leg like that it also put both revolvers almost parallel to the ground when a man was seated on a horse the way Jedediah Gable was right now. In order to keep his guns from being jostled out of the holsters and onto the ground while he was riding, a man dumb enough to carry that way had to put a thong or keeper of some sort over the hammers so as to hold them in place.

And if he wanted to drag them out, he first had to unfasten the keepers. Gable's weapons were as firmly secured inside those holsters as if he'd put them under lock and key.

"Is this a social visit, Gable? I hate t' disappoint a man as famous as you seem t' think you are, but I'm not in the mood for company right now. So ride on about your business."

"I come here to deliver a message."

"All right. Hand it here."

"It's an invite, not a letter. Miz Wesler wants to see you."

"All right. I'll stop by and call on her."

"Now."

"Tomorrow."

"She said now."

"Then she's gonna be real disappointed, because it's coming dark, I'm tired, I got coffee on the fire, and I'm gonna get some sleep. You can tell the lady I'll stop in sometime tomorrow if she'd like to have a word with me."

The woman, Longarm recalled, was said to be the matriarch of the sheepmen in Hart County. And she was the mother of the now-dead idiot who'd committed the county's last murder ten years back. Probably took herself seriously, Longarm suspected, and wanted to find out which side of the fence this newcomer was walking. That would be especially important if she was thinking about using Gable to start a war. She would certainly want to know how the opposition stacked up . . . if Longarm turned out to oppose her.

"She said to bring you," Gable insisted. "She didn't say nothing about wanting comp'ny for tea tomorra."

"Then tell her to serve coffee. And tell her I'll drop around then. Not now. Convey my regrets, hmm?"

"You're coming now, mister."

Longarm wasn't sure just exactly what Gable had in mind, but the man put the spurs to his horse and drove the animal straight at Longarm, who was standing beside his fire.

Probably intended to ride him down and rough him up, and then force him at gunpoint to go to wherever this woman lived. Well, fuck that!

Longarm took half a step to the side and grabbed the headstall of Gable's horse with one hand and its left ear with the other. The horse was moving fast when Longarm pulled its head around and yanked down.

The horse, unbalanced, toppled onto its side with Jedediah Gable still in his saddle.

Horse and man hit the ground with a loud thump and a squeal of terror from the horse.

"Dammit!"

Longarm took hold of Gable by the hair and dragged him away from the squirming, thrashing, frightened animal.

The horse scrambled to its feet and whinnied, then broke into a run toward the north.

Gable fumbled at his holster, trying to get his right-hand gun free of the restraining thong that held it fast there.

Longarm pulled Gable to his feet, still by the hair, and took hold of Gable's wrist. Longarm's fingers found the hollow between the bones of Gable's lower arm. He dug his nails in and squeezed. Hard. Jedediah Gable screamed and snatched his arm away.

That was fine by Longarm, who took the opportunity to finish pushing the hammer thong out of the way. He removed the very pretty ivory-handled Colt and tossed it aside, then spun Gable around and took his second gun too. It joined its mate in the dirt.

"You son of a bitch, you . . ."

The heel of Longarm's hand smashed upward onto the point of Gable's jaw, and the man screamed again. Bright blood began to flow out of his mouth. Probably, Longarm thought, he'd bitten off a chunk of his own tongue. Maybe busted some teeth too. Longarm wondered if Harry Sprague, the town's barber, surgeon, coroner, and undertaker, was also its dentist.

"I told you t' watch your mouth or it'd get you in trouble, didn't I?" Longarm said in a mild and pleasant tone of voice. He was very careful to make sure he was not gasping for breath after the brief little fracas, and indeed he appeared relaxed and unruffled now, while Gable was disheveled and filthy and bloody. And disarmed. The man who thought himself so tough was not coming off very well in this encounter.

"You thun of a bith," Gable mumbled.

Longarm hit him again, in the pit of his stomach. Hard. Gable doubled over and began to puke.

"Dammit," Longarm complained, "now I'm gonna have t' move my camp so's I won't be smelling your puke all night."

Of course he would have moved anyway, just to make things difficult if Gable wanted to sneak back during the night in search of revenge. But Longarm saw no point in explaining that.

"Go back," Longarm said softly, "and tell Mrs. Wesler I will be pleased to call on her tomorrow afternoon."

Gable gave him a look that Longarm thought more than a little nervous, then nodded. He turned, miserable and quite thoroughly cowed, and hobbled a few steps in the direction of his pretty guns.

"No," Longarm said. "I'll bring them with me tomorrow."

"You can'd . . . I can'd go ba' wi'oud my gunths."

"Then you can't go back at all, because I am not gonna

give them back to you tonight. Am I making myself clear here?"

"Yeth."

"What?"

"Yeth," he said a little louder.

"Yes, *what*!" Longarm demanded.

"Yeth, thir."

Longarm grunted. The proprieties had been observed. And Jedediah Jerome Gable had almost certainly spent some time in prison to have learned and so quickly acquiesced to that routine.

"Fine. Now get the hell outa my sight."

"My horth," Gable said.

"It ran off. You'll find it waiting outside its home corral, most likely."

"Ith theven mileth out there."

"What, are you afraid of the dark or something? Seven miles, hell, you'll be there in two, two and a half hours if you hoof it right along."

"I'll fuckin' kill you."

Longarm laughed. "Wash the blood off first. Then do whatever you damn please. But don't expect me to let you off so light if you ever come at me again."

Jedediah Gable turned and began limping away into the gathering dusk.

Longarm let him get out of sight before he picked up Gable's Colts and tucked them away.

Then he poured himself a cup of coffee.

Chapter 22

"It's a glorious morning, isn't it," Longarm observed as he entered the café that the woman named Maggie owned.

The daughter was there acting as waitress again. So either it was Saturday, or the little girl helped out in the mornings before she went to school. She smiled when she saw Longarm. "Yes, sir, it is. Can I bring you some coffee?"

"Please. And some of your mother's good flapjacks too."

"Cane syrup or honey?"

"Syrup, I think."

"Coming right up."

Longarm enjoyed his meal, and tipped the youngster a dime in addition to paying for the food afterward. He went outside to light a cheroot and amble over to the barbershop.

Sprague had a full house, so Longarm felt of his chin and decided his shave could wait a while. He could take advantage of that discount later on. And maybe have some privacy in which to speak with the barber about a few things while he was doing it.

In the meantime, he crossed the creek and turned the

horse over to the fellow at the livery stable, then strode back into town to find the café beside the courthouse where Terhune and his friends were said to hang out.

Adam Terhune was there, all right, seated at a long table with half-a-dozen gents, all of them dressed for the city. If these were sheepmen, they had come a long way from the days when they might've had to sleep in sheep shit.

"Aha, there. Good morning, Long. Boys, this is the fellow I've been telling you about," Terhune exclaimed, motioning for Longarm to join them.

The county commissioner mumbled a quick round of introduction—one man was named Paul, another John, beyond that Longarm was lost—then said, "And this is deputy United States Marshal Long." He waved at Longarm with a proprietary air, as if Terhune had just invented him.

So much, Longarm thought, for the idea that Terhune would keep quiet on the subject of just who Longarm was. Obviously that pledge had been forgotten before Longarm ever walked into the place this morning.

But then what could a person expect from a politician?

"My pleasure, gents."

There was no real harm done, he thought. The idea that people were being murdered here was not a real investigation to begin with, never mind what Terhune and his friends might believe. And if there really was a range war brewing, the presence of a federal peace officer just might put a damper on the notion.

Which reminded him. If Terhune was talking, Mrs. Wesler was sure to hear about it soon. Longarm wanted to have his word with her before she found out who he was. If she wanted to see him with the thought of adding another gun to her army, he wanted to know about it. And she was not likely to offer such a job to a U.S. deputy.

That meant he'd best move his visit up. He had intended to find her place this afternoon, but it looked now like morning would be the better time for it. Even without a shave.

Besides, a little beard stubble might be appropriate if she were in the market for a gunhand.

"Gents," he said to Terhune and company, "I just came by this morning to say hello and get a chance to meet you. The rest of you, that is. I had the pleasure of meeting with Commissioner Terhune yesterday. I want you to know, same as I told him, that the governor is anxious to help the good people of Hart County any way he can."

There! That took care of the bullshit out of Denver. The real part of this assignment had been taken care of, dammit. He was sure Marshal Vail would be real proud of him. If he didn't puke and once he was done laughing, that is. But then Billy felt about politics and politicians very much the same way Longarm did. The boss just had to put up with a whole hell of a lot more than his deputies did.

"Sit down, Long. Have some coffee with us," one of the sheepmen said.

"Thank you, sir. I'd enjoy nothing more, but there are some things I need to do right now. Duty, y'know. I hope you'll keep that invitation open, though."

"Any time, Long. You can find us here most mornings."

"In that case, gentlemen, please excuse me while I get about my work." He touched the brim of his Stetson. And got the hell out of there to reclaim his horse from a rather surprised hostler.

"I haven't even had a chance to groom or grain him," the fellow objected.

"I know, but something came up. I'll bring him back this afternoon so's you can finish up."

Longarm strapped his saddle back onto the bay and mounted. "Oh. There was one more thing if you don't mind. How can I find a Mrs. Martha Wesler's place?"

Chapter 23

Many of the others might have chosen to move into town and live like city folk, but Martha Wesler lived on her land. And not in any mansion either, never mind what she could afford if she chose to build a monument to herself.

The Wesler home was a low, rambling affair fashioned about half and half out of adobe mud and daub-and-wattle. It was about as squat and ugly a place as Longarm had seen since he'd last visited a Navajo hogan. On the other hand, it was comfortably cool inside. It was made of locally available materials, and would have cost only the labor that was put into it. And it quite obviously suited Martha Wexler, who answered her own door. There were sure to be servants around to help with the cooking and the cleaning, but it was the old woman herself who greeted Longarm and led him inside.

"You would be Mr. Long," she said.

"Yes, ma'am."

"You can put your hat on that rack over there."

He did so.

"You are not a bad-looking man."

"Thank you."

"I didn't so much intend a compliment, young man, as

an expression of surprise. Jedediah described you in rather unflattering terms."

Longarm only chuckled.

"No comment about why that should be so?"

"Is one necessary?"

"No, but most men like to beat their breasts and crow about their victories. You don't?"

"No." He grinned. "I suspect your man Jedediah did that for me anyhow."

"Hmmph! Not that he intended to, of course."

"No, ma'am, I wouldn't think so."

"When he first came here, Jedediah told me he couldn't be beaten by any man living."

"It was an honest mistake, I'm sure."

The old woman cackled. "I like you, Mr. Long. I surely do."

She took him into a square, low-roofed room that had a fire blazing in a beehive corner fireplace even though the day seemed plenty warm enough to Longarm.

"Sit." She pointed. "Whiskey?"

It was only mid-morning, but why not? "Sure."

She splashed heavy jolts of liquor into two crockery mugs, and kept one for herself as she settled into an armchair. "Here's mud in your eye." She tossed hers back with a practiced flick of her wrist.

Longarm took more time with his, taking the opportunity to assess the old woman over the rim of his mug.

She was not much bigger than a sparrow, but there was nothing frail about her despite her white hair and spindly limbs. She could have been any age between sixty, he thought, and, oh, a hundred eighty-five. Her dress looked like it might've been a hand-me-down from previous generations, its style ages out of date and its color lost somewhere back in time.. The dress was almost as wrinkled as Mrs. Wesler was.

She walked like she was clomping across mountain

meadows, with no hint of grace or charm. But she did not require the use of a cane or a hearing horn, and her eyes were as brightly alert as a hawk's.

"Are you done?"

"Ma'am?"

"Are you done looking me over?"

"Yes, thank you." He grinned at her and tried the whiskey. It came out of a plain jug and was served in a crockery mug with chips around the rim . . . and it was as smooth and fine a drink as he could remember having.

His surprise must have showed, because Mrs. Wesler began to laugh. "What's money for if not to enjoy, young man?"

"I like your attitude," he said.

"And I like yours," she countered. "But let's not beat around the bush, shall we? You know why I wanted to see you, I suppose."

"I can think of a couple possible reasons, but I'll let you do the talking since you're the only one as knows the certain sure truth."

"Why, I want to know your business here, of course. I want to know if those dirt-farming sons of bitches are planning a war against us. If they are the ones who brought you here, I intend to hire you away from them. I'll double whatever they promised. More important than that, I'll put you on the winning side."

"If, that is, it comes to a fight," he said.

"Mr. Long, have you seen the ditch they're digging over yonder?"

"Yes, ma'am, I have."

"Then you know it will come to a fight. Sooner or later we will have to work out which of us will prevail here. My suggestion to you, Mr. Long, is that you align yourself with the eventual winner."

"And my answer to you, Mrs. Wesler, is that if I was

t' pick a side . . . and mind you I'm saying 'if' . . . then that side would surely come out the winner."

"So. You aren't always modest and shy about yourself, are you?"

"You saw your champion feist dog when he got home last night. D'you think I need to be self-effacing and falsely modest? I'm good at what I do, Mrs. Wesler. I'll go so far as to tell you that I am very good at what I do. That's something both you sheep folks and the farmers over there might wanta keep in mind over this next little while."

"I don't know whether to redouble my intention to hire you, Mr. Long . . . or have Jedediah shoot you."

"If you choose the latter, ma'am, then I expect you'd best remind him t' do it from ambush. That's the only way he'd ever be able t' get that job done."

"Hire you," she said. "I have decided. Name your price, sir. I am a rich woman in my own right, and if I have to, I will get the others to pitch in with the price of your hire. Just tell me what that price will be."

"The price to keep me from coming after you," Longarm said after another sip of the excellent whiskey, "is peace."

"What was that?"

"I've already been hired, ma'am, but not by the farmers." He set the mug aside and reached inside his coat for the the wallet and badge he carried there.

"There isn't gonna be any range war," he said as he pulled them out. "Mark my words about that, ma'am. You folks can fight all you like at the ballot box, but I'll not allow any gun talk."

He flipped the wallet open and showed her why he said that.

Chapter 24

Damn if he didn't purely like that old woman, Longarm thought as he rode back to Weirville. She was honest. That was not something that could be said of everyone. Of course she was also mean as a damn snake, and wouldn't bat an eye over little matters like killing someone who opposed her. But he liked her.

Since the rag was completely off the bush now about who he was—even if there would still remain a certain amount of confusion about *why* he was here, some continuing to think it had to do with Commissioner Terhune's fears about phantom murders—he supposed he should go and introduce himself a little more properly to the sheriff, then spend some time with the town barber.

He took the bay back to the livery, where the hostler greeted him with; "Are you gonna leave that animal long enough this time so's I can get him properly tended?"

"Yes, sir." Longarm unfastened his cinches and pulled his saddle.

"Mind now. If you come back here in ten minutes thinking you're gonna interrupt me again, I'm not letting you have the horse. Not till I'm done with him. Do you hear me, young man?"

"Yes, sir, I do."

"All right then. Now whereat are you headed for this time that I have to give you direction?"

Longarm laughed. "I know where I'm heading now."

"For a change," the hostler grumbled.

"You've been a big help."

"Huh!" he snorted. But he looked pleased with the idea that someone appreciated him.

It was lunchtime, and he did not expect to find Bill Thompson at the jail at this hour, so Longarm went back to the café beside the courthouse rather than walk across to the farmers' side of town and the restaurant where he had been taking his meals here.

This time the long table at the back where the prosperous sheepmen had their informal gatherings was occupied by a half-dozen men in sleeve garters and low-cut shoes. Longarm guessed them to be county employees from across the street.

The woman who ran the café was in her mid-to-late forties, or so he guessed. She was beginning to get some streaks of gray in her hair, and her hands and neck carried the telltale wrinkles of impending age. She looked sickly, he thought. And unhappy. None of the customers joked or teased with her, and she did not smile when speaking with them. Longarm found nothing odd about not receiving a warm welcome himself since he was, after all a stranger here and not known to her. But it seemed sad that she would hold herself so far apart from people she likely knew long and well. He suspected she once had been a pretty woman, but time and a gloomy outlook seemed to have leached that away from her over the years.

"You want coffee?" was her greeting.

"Yes, please."

"Sit anyplace. You want today's special?"

"That will be fine, thank you."

She turned and disappeared into a side room where the

kitchen must be. Longarm could not help noting the contrast between this eatery and the one where Maggie and her bubbly daughter held forth on the other side of the creek. He suspected if the sheepmen ever found out how pleasant it was over there, this woman—what was her name again? Terhune had mentioned it . . . oh yes, Hilda—if the sheepmen ever made that discovery, poor poor Hilda would probably find herself out of business and never mind the convenience of her courthouse square location.

She delivered his coffee along with a can of condensed milk and a nearly empty bowl of light brown sugar. She put them down and departed without a word. Yep. Friendly, he thought. Real welcoming to a new customer.

The coffee was good, though. Hot and fresh. That was something to her credit. And the meal, quickly delivered, was also hot and fresh.

It was also, dammit, a mutton stew. Longarm did *not* like the heavy flavor of mutton. Lamb was fine. Delicate and tasty. But mutton . . . he scowled. It was his own damn fault, he supposed, for not asking what the day's special was.

Could be, he thought as he dug a spoon in for a second mouthful, that a steady diet of mutton was the reason Hilda was so glum. He knew he damn sure would be if he had to put up with mutton day in and day out. Why, the smell of it cooking would be enough to turn a man's stomach. And having to eat it too? He was glad now that he spent most of his time in cow country. There isn't hardly any way you can mess up the taste of beef, not until it's gotten so bad the maggots don't want it.

"Deputy?"

He looked up to see Sheriff Thompson standing there. "You've already heard that obviously."

"Uh-huh."

"I was on my way over to the courthouse to find you.

Figured you'd be off t' lunch now, though. Sit down. Let me buy you some of this stew." He smiled. "I assume you do eat mutton."

Hilda appeared at Thompson's elbow. "Your usual?"

"Yes, please." Hilda left, and Thompson helped himself to a chair across the table from Longarm.

"What's your usual? Not the mutton?"

"I know it makes the sheep faction think I'm making a political statement by it, and I regret that, but the truth is that I just don't like mutton. I always order the fried sage hen. Hilda does a bang-up job with sage hen."

Longarm groaned. "If only I'd known."

Thompson smiled. "Now tell me. You really are a federal officer? That's what I heard a little while ago."

Longarm nodded, and for the second time that day pulled out his wallet.

Chapter 25

"I can't believe you're going to investigate Adam's crazy notion that folks are being murdered here," the young sheriff said.

Longarm looked at Thompson for a moment, then told himself what the hell. Some things are serious. Others aren't. "You and me don't know each other, Sheriff. . . ."

"Call me Bill."

"All right. An' you can call me Longarm if you like. Most o' my friends do."

"Long*arm*? You're *that* deputy? Hell, man, you're practically famous."

"Which will buy a man a beer if he adds a nickel to it. Anyway, Bill, what I was fixing to say is that we aren't real well acquainted yet, but there's a couple things I'd like to tell you just between the two of us."

"I can keep my mouth shut, Longarm." He grinned. "Except at supper time, that is."

"I'm here, Bill, because the governor asked the U.S. Attorney to ask the U.S. marshal to assign one of his people to what everybody knows is a bullshit case. It's all politics, Bill. The governor is obviously wanting something from the Hart County delegation at the capital, and

I'm the unlucky idjit who happened to be available. There's no crime in a death by natural causes and that's that, never mind what Commissioner Terhune thinks."

"All right. I can understand that," the Hart County sheriff said. "So you intend to make a show of being here. Talk to some people. Make the commissioners happy . . . which reminds me, when you get back to Denver, Longarm, you might want to mention to the governor that come the next election he will be dealing with county commissioners and legislators from a different camp than the fellows he's known before."

"Aw, he'll find out without me mixing into it," Longarm said. "I care about enforcing the laws. I don't much give a shit what happens when it comes to politics. If only because there's so awful few politicians worth the powder it would take to blow their miserable asses to Hell."

"Careful what you say here. I happen to've been elected to office myself, you know," Thompson said. His voice, though, was cheerful and his eyes laughing.

"Yeah, well, everybody has crosses to bear. I expect having to walk around knowing you're sucking a public tit is yours. But Bill, there is something serious I need t' mention to you now that I've found out about it."

Thompson's eyebrows went up. He remained silent and waited for Longarm to continue.

"This morning old Mrs. Wesler tried to hire me, Bill. As a gunhand."

"What would she . . . oh, shit. She's gonna start a range war?"

"I can't say that she is or that she isn't," Longarm told him. "We didn't get down to specifics, you understand. She thought the farmers brought me in here as a paid gun to back their side o' things, and she offered to hire me away. Said she'd outbid them no matter what money they'd promised."

"She has money enough to do it too, I would think."

"And this isn't only her play, Bill. She also said she could draw on the resources of the other sheepmen if she had to."

"I don't like the sound of that."

"Didn't reckon you would. It's just lucky it came out now, before that son of a bitch Gable got to running roughshod over people."

"Gable?" Thompson frowned and shook his head. "Who is Gable and what does he have to do with this?"

"You didn't know Mrs. Wesler already hired herself a killer?"

"A killer? Christ, no. Are you sure?"

"The man's a bully as well as a killer, Bill. Fancies himself a hard man. I expect he could back that up against some poor dirt farmer with only a hoe to defend himself." Longarm told the sheriff about his own run-in with Jedediah Jerome Gable, lately of Arizona Territory.

The sheriff's frown deepened. "This Gable might not find it as easy to intimidate these farmers as he expects. A good many of them, most of them perhaps, fought in the recent war, and while they may not be well versed when it comes to belly guns and gunfighting, I'd say pretty much all of them could reach over their door frame and take down a rifle or a shotgun. And know what to do with it once they did."

"If they had time enough to do that, Bill. I don't think you could count on Gable to make a fair fight of it. And anyway, what's needed here is not for the farmers to fight well, but for you . . . and me if I can help out . . . to see that there's no fighting to be done. I already told Mrs. Wesler that she'd best keep this contest confined to the voting booth and forget about gun smoke. Course I got no way to know if she'll take that excellent advise. But I damn sure hope she will."

"You've given me a lot to think about, Longarm."

"At least you have a warning ahead of time, Bill. You want some advice from me?"

"I'd welcome it."

"Look up this Jedediah Gable. Take your handcuffs and beat him until his face isn't nothing but raw meat, then stomp him until he'll piss blood for the next month and a half. And once you've got him in a mood to listen to you, let him know that he's free to do whatever he wants, but your suggestion to him would be that Arizona is a lot healthier place for him to be. In other words, run his ragged ass plumb out of this county and tell him to not so much as look back until he's two days beyond the county line. That's what I'd do if I was you, Bill."

"What you're suggesting is illegal as hell, Longarm."

"You could look at it that you're defending the peace and public order. Which, in fact, you would be."

Thompson shook his head. "You wouldn't handle Gable that way if you were sheriff here, Longarm. I've heard too much about you to believe that."

"Maybe so, Bill, but then I know I could put three slugs in Gable's belly before his gun ever cleared leather. More t' the point, now Jedediah Gable knows that I could too. I could spit in his face an' tell him to lick it clean an' he still wouldn't draw against me. What about you, Bill? Ever face anybody in a stand-up, face-to-face shootout? Ever kill anybody? Hell, have you ever drawn your gun and *pointed* it at anyone?"

"All right, no. I haven't. But that doesn't mean that I couldn't."

"No, and for all I know, Bill, you could even beat Gable in a fair fight. After all, I've never seen either one of you in action. But that isn't really the point. A lawman's main job isn't to shoot people. It's to keep the peace. To *keep* it, Bill. An' anything you have t' do to keep Jedediah Gable from using his gun . . . on you or on me or on any citizen of this county . . . is your duty t' do."

"I never . . . you've given me a lot to think about, Longarm. And I don't know whether I should thank you for it or cuss you."

"Prob'ly you oughta do some of each. But at least you got some advance warning about troubles yet to come. I hope that will do some good for you an' the folks hereabouts." Longarm dropped money on the table to pay for both meals, then picked up his Stetson and said his good-byes to a very solemn and pensive county sheriff.

Chapter 26

There was one man in Harry Sprague's barber chair when Longarm arrived, and another already waiting, so Longarm settled down to wait his turn. He picked up a copy of the *Police Gazette*, which was his favorite reading . . . whenever he wanted a laugh. The *Gazette* seemed to take itself mighty seriously, but Longarm never could.

The tabloid was filled with wildly imaginative but totally preposterous stories that pretended to be news, and its articles were rife with inaccuracy and speculation. The writers knew how to concoct a stirring tale, he conceded, but they knew nothing about horses, guns, cowboying, or law enforcement. None of which kept them from holding forth as if they were experts on any and every subject. Longarm read the *Gazette* every chance he got. It never failed to amuse, even if it did fall short when it came to informing.

Sprague quickly finished the shave he was working on, and that customer left the shop while the next man in line crawled onto the chair and closed his eyes for a light snooze while Sprague trimmed his hair and gave him a shave. Another man came in while that one was being attended to. When Longarm's turn came he motioned for the latecomer to go ahead, holding up the pages of the *Gazette* by way of explanation.

Sprague finished with the man and nodded for Longarm to take the chair next.

"Thanks," Longarm said. But instead of getting into the chair, he first went to the door to flip the *Open* sign around so from the outside it read *Closed*. Then he pulled the blind over the front and door windows.

"If I hadn't heard you're a deputy United States marshal, I think I'd be worried right now about maybe being robbed. You, uh, *are* a deputy marshal, aren't you?" the barber asked.

Longarm smiled. "Yes, sir, and I'm not gonna rob you. But I am gonna ask you a few questions if you don't mind."

"That's fine, but would it be possible for us to get together this evening after I close the shop?" Sprague suggested. "I have three regulars who will be coming by in the next half hour or so, and I don't want to disappoint them unless it is really necessary. Would that be all right with you, Marshal?"

"Y'know, I shoulda thought of that my own self. I'm sorry." Longarm raised both blinds again and turned the sign back around to show the shop was open for business. He smiled. "Reckon it is my turn in the chair, though, and I'm needing that cut-rate shave you promised."

"No sooner said than done."

While he shaved Longarm he gave directions to his house and said, "I close down here about six, then stop and have supper and maybe a drink or two afterward. Why don't you come by, oh, let's say eight o'clock or so. That will give me time to get home and take my shoes off. Would that be all right with you?"

"Of course. I'll try and be prompt."

"All right then. Eight it is."

Sprague finished with the shave and Longarm paid

him—full price—before reclaiming his hat and heading outside into the mid-afternoon sunshine.

He had a fair number of hours to kill before eight o'clock and no place he really needed to be until then.

When a situation like that arose . . .

Longarm grinned and began striding at a rapid clip toward the livery stable, where by now his horse should be available without the hostler refusing to turn it over.

He hoped Sissy Beckham wasn't so awfully busy this afternoon because she was about to receive a visit from a tall, horny gent.

Chapter 27

There were no public hitching rails on the residential street and no trees to tie to, so Longarm secured his horse to a corner post on the rather rickety fence in front of Harry Sprague's house. He felt pretty good after his afternoon of . . . relaxation . . . at the Beckham orchard. Damned good, in fact. He had spent the bulk of the afternoon in bed. Then Sissy had compounded his pleasure by cooking supper before he had to leave.

It was still early enough in the year that he had only twilight remaining by the time he got back to town—more or less on time—for his meeting with Barber Sprague. In a few more months it would still be broad daylight, or close to it, at this hour, but for now the light was diminishing quickly.

Sprague was standing at the door by the time Longarm finished securing the horse and let himself in through the front gate. "Right on time," the barber said. Longarm had an impulse to drag out his key-wound Ingersoll and check that, but resisted it and accepted Sprague's statement. It did surprise him, though, as he hadn't been paying all that much mind to the hour.

Sprague pushed the door open, and Longarm entered a

small but tidy and comfortably furnished home. There were curtains at the windows and framed pieces of fancy embroidery on the walls. Longarm removed his hat and asked, "Is your missus out tonight?"

"I'm a widower, Marshal. My wife died a good many years ago, God rest her soul. She was a good woman. I keep thinking I'll get over missing her, but I don't."

"I'm sorry t' hear that."

Sprague shrugged. "We do with what we have, right?"

"Right." Longarm wasn't entirely sure he agreed with that philosophy—after all, there were some things a man could change—but it wasn't something he wanted to argue about.

"Come in. Have a seat. I'll go fetch us some coffee. You'll have a cup with me, I hope."

"Sounds fine, thank you."

Sprague went toward the back of the house where the kitchen would obviously be, and Longarm chose a chair in the parlor. There was a sofa that looked too low for comfort, and a rather large armchair with a footstool in front of it. That would be Sprague's own easy chair, Longarm figured, and he did not want to intrude on that.

The barber returned a couple minutes later carrying a small tray with two slightly overfull cups on it and a matched set of creamer and sugar serving bowls. There was coffee sloshing around in the tray as well as in the cups. Not quite all of it had made it from the kitchen still in the cups.

"Milk? Sugar?"

"I'm fine, thanks." Longarm accepted one of the cups, and carefully wiped the bottom of the saucer on his trousers before putting it down on the little table beside his chair lest it leave a ring on the wood.

"Is the breeze too cold on your neck there?" Sprague asked.

"It is getting t' be a mite chill now that the sun's down."

The barber put the tray down close to his own chair, then slid the window shut-behind Longarm. "There. That's better." He sat and picked up his cup. "Now. How can I be of help, Marshal?"

Harry Sprague was pleasant. Open. Cooperative. Friendly as he could be. He could not, naturally enough, give information about anyone being murdered in or around Weirville in these past couple years.

Yes, he remembered each death quite well.

Yes, in addition to everything else, he did act as undertaker and had provided the burial arrangements. No embalming, though. He did not have either the equipment or the expertise to do that. The best he could manage was to wash and lay out the departed, prepare a coffin to fit, and oversee the actual interment.

No, he hadn't been called to provide medical care for any of the dead in those cases Adam Terhune found so suspicious. "But I did know they were sick. In fact, Ben Evans came to me after he came down with whatever this flux was. He asked me for some ipecac, which I gave him. Though it was beyond me why he would want ipecac when it was a general debility and loss of vitality that he claimed he was having."

"Ipecac. That's the stuff that makes you puke, isn't it?"

"That's right, it is. Brings up everything you've eaten for days past. Your toenails too if you take too much of it. Like I say, that's what Ben asked for, so that's what I gave him. Could be he intended it for something other than the illness he was feeling right then. I wouldn't know about that since he didn't offer to tell me and I didn't ask."

"Did you notice anything peculiar about the dead when you were laying them out?"

"You mean like wounds or . . . I don't know . . . bleeding from the ears or something of that sort?"

"Bleeding from the ears?"

Sprague smiled. "I may be a country bumpkin and just a barber, Marshal, but I can read. I know about murdering somebody by poking a knitting needle or crochet hook into the ear so it doesn't leave a visible wound. I read about things like that, and I like to think I wouldn't overlook such evidence if any ever came before me. But there wasn't anything at all like that on these men. Each of them came down sick and eventually died. Far as I could tell, that's all there was to it."

"You say 'eventually.' How long would you say they were sick before they, uh, expired?"

"Hmm. Now mind, I wasn't called to care for them so I can't say with any certainty. But in a town this size you tend to hear things, and everybody knew they were sick well before they died. I'd guess they must've been off their feet a good two weeks before they died. And off their feed for a week or two before that, but not sick enough to take to bed with it."

"Three, four weeks total then?" Longarm asked.

"Something like that, yes."

"So it wasn't anything real sudden."

"No. And I know you've been asked to look into these deaths as murders, Marshal, but I really can't see that they were. Folks get sick. Folks die. It's the way of things. I never saw anything that would make me think any single one of those men was murdered. I certainly don't think they all were."

"You're very helpful, Mr. Sprague."

The barber shrugged. "I'm willing, Marshal. I just don't have anything to tell you that would be helpful."

"The truth is all I want from any man, sir."

"Well, I can give you that anyway. Would you like more coffee?"

"No, thank you." Harry Sprague was a very nice man. But he did not make very good coffee. Too weak for Longarm's taste. "I'll finish this and get out of your way. But I truly do thank you."

"Any time, Marshal, I . . ."

Whatever Sprague intended to say was lost in an explosion of flying glass and the thud of a bullet striking something solid.

The back of Longarm's chair jerked and the curtain at the window behind him billowed.

Longarm found himself kneeling in front of the shattered window with his Colt in hand.

The assassin's bullet had plowed into the back of the chair instead of striking Longarm's head, which was undoubtedly the target it was intended for.

Chapter 28

"It was the glass," Longarm said.

"Pardon me? What do you mean? What was the glass?"

"The glass in the window. The stuff is brittle, but it can be enough to deflect the flight of a bullet if the impact isn't straight on. My bet is that whoever fired that shot did so from an angle. The change in the course of that slug was enough to put it into the chair.

"I'm grateful that it did, o' course. I'll make it good to you about the window and the damage to your chair."

"Forget about the chair. I can just sew up the hole in the upholstery. That will be all right. If you want to help, buy me another pane of glass. Tom Benjamin carries glass at the hardware store. Costs a lot, though, because it's so hard to get a piece in here unbroken after being bounced around on the roads."

"I'll take care of it first thing tomorrow, Mr. Sprague. I'm truly sorry it happened."

"Far sorrier than I am, I'd say," the barber/doctor/undertaker said. "After all, I just lost a window. You could've lost your life."

"Excuse me. Sir? Excuse me, please?"

They were standing on the street in front of Sprague's

house. Longarm hadn't made much of an effort to find the would-be assassin. Whoever it was had had more than enough time to slip away into the young night before Longarm could get outside.

Longarm's conversation with Sprague was interrupted by the arrival of a woman wearing a hooded cloak to fend off the chill of the evening. She was carrying a basket.

"Was it you he shot at?" she asked now.

"Ma'am?"

"I was on my way home. I saw someone standing over there." She pointed. "I thought he was . . . oh, dear, I hate having to utter such a thing . . . but I thought he was, well, relieving himself. Naturally I turned my eyes away. Then I heard the shot and . . . and . . . there was a flash of light. Like a fire flaring up. And when I turned to see, the man was running away. Into the alley. Back there." She pointed again.

"Who was it, ma'am?"

"I didn't look at him closely. I would not, of course, under those circumstances, thinking what I thought he was doing, I mean."

"No, ma'am, of course you would not. What can you tell me about him? What was he wearing? How tall was he? What color hair did he have? What . . . ?"

"Wait. Please. I really can't tell you much of anything. I did not get a proper look at him. Mostly what I recall is . . . an impression, I suppose you would say. He was not overly tall, I think. Lightly built. He was wearing . . . oh, dear, it is so difficult to remember." She paused, then after a moment shrugged. "Dark clothing. I'm sorry. I really can't tell you beyond that."

"Was he wearing a coat? Or was he in shirtsleeves? Did he have a hat? What shape was it?"

"I don't . . . oh, I am so very sorry, but I just cannot recall. I'm sorry."

"Yes, ma'am."

"Miss. It is 'miss' if you please, sir. Miss Hilda Wannamacher."

"All right, Miss Wann . . ." Longarm snapped his fingers. "You are the lady who runs the café by the courthouse, aren't you?"

"Yes, of course."

"My apologies, Miss Wannamacher. I didn't recognize you with your hood and cape."

"That is quite all right, sir. You are a newcomer. One could not expect you to know everyone yet."

Longarm smiled. "Reckon I never will either. I don't expect to be around all that long." He introduced himself.

"So you will be leaving as soon as you apprehend the murderer?" she asked.

"I would expect to, yes." He couldn't see any point in announcing to her or anybody else that there was no murderer because there had been no murders.

And yet . . .

Why in hell had some son of a bitch shot at him tonight if there was no . . .

He grunted and snapped his fingers again. Jedediah Jerome Gable.

It was his own damn fault, he supposed. He'd told Mrs. Wesler that Gable's only chance was to shoot him from ambush.

And damned if the son of a bitch hadn't gone and done it.

"Miss Wannamacher, thank you. You've been a big help to me."

"Have I? Oh, I am so glad to know that. I abhor violence of any kind. Guns, fighting." She shuddered. "It is all so ugly."

"Yes, ma'am . . . excuse me . . . miss . . . yes, it really is ugly. I'm sorry you had to witness it. May I ask you, please, if you think of anything else, any tiny detail at all, please tell either me or Sheriff Thompson. Would you do that, please?"

"Of course. I shall think about it this evening and if I call anything else to mind, I will be sure to let you know about it immediately."

"T'morrow mornin' would be plenty soon enough, miss. Thank you."

Miss Wannamacher resumed her journey, basket over her arm and hood keeping her features in shadow, while Longarm and Sprague went back inside. Longarm needed to get another look at that window so he would know what size piece of glass would be needed to replace it.

And he hoped Mr. Sprague would not be too upset, but Longarm intended to do still more damage to the chair he'd been sitting in. The bullet that struck it had not passed through the upholstery on the front side. Longarm intended to dig the slug out and see if there was anything it could tell him.

Chapter 29

"I'm sorry, Longarm," the young sheriff said. "We've checked every saloon and billiard parlor on both sides of the creek, and Frenchie's here is the only whorehouse we have in the county."

"He could be with some independent whore, I suppose," Longarm said thoughtfully. "I'm sure you have some of those."

"Of course we do, but they all work out of the saloons, and no one at any of those has seen Gable tonight."

"Amateurs maybe?" Longarm asked. He knew he was grasping at straws, but he asked it anyway. He was more than just a little peeved with Jedediah Gable, and looked forward to an opportunity to put that son of a bitch behind bars. Assault on a federal officer was considered impolite in some quarters . . . and damned well illegal in others. Longarm intended to take the man back to Denver and prosecute him for that wayward gunshot.

In fact, Longarm would be pleased to take Gable away in irons and prosecute him even if he could find no evidence that Gable fired the shot. After all, that would very effectively take him out of Hart County and help keep a lid on the peace that now existed between the sheep and farming factions here.

"My advice," Thompson said, "would be for us to wait until daylight, then ride out to the Wesler place. If Gable isn't getting drunk or getting laid, he's probably in the bunkhouse playing cards. We can leave early and catch him at breakfast."

"Unless he's skeedaddled. But I suppose that would be all right too. It'd get him out of your hair."

"To tell you the truth, Longarm, I thought about that too. I can think of worse things than seeing Gable's hairy ass cross the horizon. Where would you like me to meet you come morning?"

"It's good o' you to offer, Bill, but there's no need for that. I can bring Gable in on my own without you having to shake out early. Me, I'm always awake before dawn anyhow. And I've no idea where I'll want t' stay tonight. No need for me t' sleep on the ground now that everybody knows who I am." He smiled. "I can use an expense voucher now an' make sure everything comes outa Uncle Sam's pocket an' not mine."

"Would you like a suggestion?"

"Sure."

"Hilda Wannamacher takes in boarders. And she's a good enough cook. I'm told anybody staying with her gets his meals thrown in at the café free of charge. Plus you know she's still awake."

"I don't know where she lives."

"It's in the next block from my place. Come along. I'll show you."

The scent of coffee boiling over an open fire. The sight of stars gleaming bright in the dark canopy of the heavens. The warmth of a campfire fending off the chill of night. Yes, sir, those are wonderful things, the sort of of things poets wax poetically about. Right.

Truth was, none of that can compete with a mattress and clean sheets when it comes to getting a good rest.

And there has never been a creek made yet that will compare with a china basin and pitcher of warm water for washing up in the morning.

Longarm slept better that night than he had since he left home. Come morning, he felt refreshed and ready. No aches. No pains. No complaints about anything.

"You're up mighty early," he said when he came downstairs and found Miss Wannamacher already awake and busying about in her home kitchen. She was elbow-deep in a huge bowl of white flour and some wet ingredients.

"I have to get my biscuit dough prepared. I'll let it set for a while, then do my baking at the restaurant, but I like to do the mixing here. That gives me a little more time in the mornings."

"Makes sense," he said. "That's a mighty heavy-looking bowl. How's about I carry it over to the café for you."

"Why, that is very nice of you to offer, Marshal. Thank you." She damn near managed a smile, he saw. And that seemed to be something she very rarely did. She had that pinched, sour look of a confirmed and lifelong pessimist.

"Whenever you're ready then."

"I won't be but a few minutes. Sit down there. I can't offer you coffee. I never make it at home. I prefer tea myself. But I'll be putting a pot on to boil as soon as we reach the restaurant."

"I'm fine, thank you. Tell you what, though. I'll step out back for a few minutes while you're finishing up here."

She nodded, and continued kneading her dough.

Longarm went out to the backhouse for a peaceful—and comfortable—morning shit, that being something else in which civilized surroundings beat hell out of a camp in the woods. He smoked a leisurely cheroot and washed at the stand beside the back door. When he returned to Miss Wannamacher's kitchen, she was done with the biscuit dough. She had a towel draped over the bowl, and was busy plucking small boxes and vials out of a wall cabinet and dropping them into the pocket of her apron. Spices she'd be wanting during the day, he supposed.

He carried the bowl—it was a heavy sonuvabitch, and it amazed him that she would do this by herself morning after morning—to the café, and waited while she unlocked the door and let them in.

She made swift and practiced work of lighting the lamps on the walls and getting a fire started in the big cast-iron range in the kitchen. The fire had been laid the night before, so all it took was a touch of a sulphur-tipped lucifer to get a blaze crackling.

"Can I fill the reservoir for you, miss?"

"Thank you, but I always do that before I leave in the evening. Just sit down and relax. I'll have your breakfast ready before you know it."

She was as good as her word. She had coffee, biscuits, bacon, and bacon gravy in front of him in less time than he would have imagined. The biscuits were excellent and, hell, there isn't much anybody can do to screw up bacon and a simple gravy. But her coffee just wasn't near as good as he could get across the creek. This morning it had something of a bitter undertaste to it that he couldn't identify. Something in the water probably. He sniffed. It didn't smell like there was anything dead floating in the hot-water reservoir, so he kept his mouth shut and drank the coffee.

It was still well short of daybreak when he retrieved the bay horse from the livery stable and headed off toward Martha Wesler's sheep ranch.

Chapter 30

It was full daylight when Longarm reached the Wesler place, and all the hands—shepherds? whatever the hell you called sheep ranch employees hereabouts—were all off doing whatever it was they did. Which, according to all the jokes on the subject, was something best left unexplored. Unless a fellow was really, *really* horny.

Longarm did manage to locate a small, slender, dark little man who looked Mexican but whose accent was not Spanish. Something close, though. Basque, Longarm assumed. "I tell him," the little fellow said when Longarm inquired about Gable. "He sleeping."

"All right, thanks."

"You see Missy Wez'er?"

"Not today," Longarm said.

The Basque shrugged and went into a small outbuilding separate from the bunkhouse, where the commoners lived. Longarm guessed that Jedediah the Great—in his own mind anyway—did not intend to be housed with a bunch of low-class sheep-chasers.

Or it could be that they were sensible enough that they did not want him around them.

In any event, Longarm left his horse tied close to the

cookhouse and trailed along behind the helpful Basque, waiting for Gable to show himself.

"He come soon," the sheepherder said when he emerged from Gable's makeshift private quarters.

"All right, thanks." Longarm lighted a cheroot and leaned against the rails of a corral fence. The corral was empty at the moment, but the hoof-churned mud surrounding the water trough suggested it had been in active use until the workers left this morning. Wheel tracks nearby added the information that they seemed to be traveling in wagons instead of on horseback. And there didn't seem to be but a very few of them.

Of course, he recalled, sheep wranglers tend to live and work with their bands of roving sheep while other wagons carry supplies to them from time to time. It could very likely be that what they had here at the headquarters was only the group of men who tended to the needs of the sheep tenders. That made sense to him. He considered asking the Basque fellow about it.

But then Jed Gable appeared in the low doorway of the shack where he was bunking, and Longarm put all thoughts of sheep aside.

"You son of a bitch!" Gable roared.

"Funny," Longarm said. "I was just gonna say somethin' on that order my own self. You're under arrest, Gable. Take that gunbelt off. Turn around. Stand easy while I put the manacles on you."

"Arrest, hell. What for?"

"Assault on a federal peace officer," Longarm said. "Your tough luck and my good that you missed last night."

"Missed what?"

"I'm not gonna debate with you about this," Longarm told him. "Now drop the gunbelt and put your hands in back. But turn around first. I don't want t' take a chance that you carry that little .32 in the small o' your back."

"What the fuck are you talking about, mister? And what's this shit about a .32? I wouldn't be caught dead with some little piece of shit like a .32, puny little pipsqueak-thing."

"Bullshit, Gable. It was a .32 slug that I dug out of that chair last night. What was it, you wanted to keep the noise of the gunshot down? Or you thought no one would think a big, tough asshole like you would carry such a puny popgun?"

"I don't know what you're talking about," Gable insisted.

"Like I said, I didn't come here to argue with you. I came here to place you under arrest."

"You can kiss my ass, bub. You aren't arresting me, and that's that." Gable straightened his shoulders and squared his stance.

Very deliberately the Arizona bad boy reached down and slipped the retaining thong off the hammer of his .45.

"If you make a move toward that gun, Gable, you aren't gonna like what happens next."

"Oh, I think I'll like it just fine, asshole."

"Let it go, Gable. I came here to arrest you, not to kill you."

"Mister, you ain't killing nobody today."

Jedediah Gable threw his left hand high in the air—a ploy intended to distract his opponent perhaps, or a sort of counterbalance to the movement of the right hand? Longarm would never know. Instantly Gable clutched the grips of his revolver with his right hand.

Longarm palmed his Colt and shot Gable in the chest. The bullet shattered his breastbone and sent a spray of lead and bone through the chest cavity, exploding the heart and instantly paralyzing the whole body.

He could see in Gable's eyes that he still lived for half a second or so. Long enough to know that he'd been killed. Long enough to know that his last words were grievously wrong.

His eyes went wide with shocked surprise. And then the light of life flickered out, and his eyes became dull and empty.

Jedediah Gable dropped to his knees and toppled face-forward onto the hard Colorado ground.

His gun remained secure in its holster. It had never cleared leather.

"Reckon those old boys in Arizona are a slower bunch than I was givin' them credit for if you was one o' the best down there," Longarm muttered to a man who no longer could hear him.

"How very foolish," Martha Wesler said. "How very stupidly wasteful."

"Yes, ma'am, I reckon it was at that. He wouldn't've spent more than five, six years in the federal pen. Now he's got no years t' spend anyplace."

"No, you don't understand at all what I was saying there, Marshal."

"I don't, ma'am?"

"Whatever you may believe, I can assure you that the late Mr. Gable most emphatically did not fire a shot at you last evening."

"I don't think I understand you, ma'am."

"I had a gathering of my colleagues last night. All the major sheepmen were here at my place. We discussed . . . shall I say . . . affairs of common interest."

"Yes, ma'am?"

"Mr. Gable was at my side the entire evening, Marshal. Here. In my dining room. With a dozen witnesses who can corroborate his presence. I can assure you that he never left my house until past midnight last night, and I am quite certain he did not go anywhere after that or I surely would have heard him leave. I sleep very lightly,

Marshal. Mr. Gable was *not* the man who shot at you."

"Shit!" Longarm said. "Uh, begging your pardon, ma'am."

"Under the circumstances, I don't blame you. Would you like another shot of that coffee? Perhaps without the actual coffee this time?"

"Yes, ma'am, maybe I will at that."

Chapter 31

"If Jedediah Gable didn't take that shot at you last night, Longarm, who the hell did?" the sheriff asked.

"Funny thing. Bill. I was gonna ask you the same thing. D'you have any fugitives hereabouts? Anybody who'd get nervous at the thought of a federal officer runnin' loose in the woods?"

"If I knew of any they wouldn't still be fugitives. I'd have them in jail or else ship them off to wherever they're wanted," Thompson said. "I don't even have any parolees in the county. We just don't have much in the way of serious crime here. Well, at least we didn't until last night."

Longarm grunted. "And with a .32. Know of anybody carries a .32? I can tell you that Gable didn't. I went through every piece o' his gear and practically tore up that shack he was living in. He had his regular revolvers an' a Kennedy lever-action carbine in .45–60, but no hide-out gun at all. Not a derringer, nothing."

"I'm sure there are plenty of .32's sitting around in cash boxes or dresser drawers in bedrooms. That is the sort of thing they're useful for. But I wouldn't have any way to know about any of those."

"I think maybe after lunch I'll wander around an' talk to the merchants. See if they can recall anybody buying .32 cartridges. That might point me in a direction."

"It's worth a try," Thompson said, sounding like he did not believe that statement for a moment. Well, that was reasonable. Longarm didn't believe it either, but you don't learn unless you look. He would try it no matter how unlikely it was the effort would succeed.

"Speaking of lunch," Thompson added, "I take it you'll be having yours at Hilda's place?"

Longarm nodded. "The government's paying to board me. No sense buying one meal twice. Care t' join me?"

"That's why I asked." The young sheriff grinned. "I can be a very subtle fellow, you know."

"Come along then, Bill."

They walked across the street from the sheriff's courthouse office to the café, where the usual crowd of public employees was having their lunch. This time Longarm knew to ask for the prairie chicken, though, rather than put up with the flavor of mutton the rest of the afternoon.

Longarm and Thompson ate mostly in silence, then leaned back to enjoy their coffee afterward.

"I'm wondering what effect the loss of Gable will have on the sheepmen's plans," the sheriff said. "I hope it will be enough to put them off that track. They're not violent men, you see. It's change they are resisting, not really the farmers at all. And now that they no longer have a hired bully to do the dirty work . . . I'm hoping the whole thing will die down and fade away of its own accord."

"Could happen, I suppose," Longarm said. "I hope it does. It all depends on Miz Wesler, I'd say. She's the one brought Gable in here. Be up to her if she looks for a replacement."

"I'm spoiled, Longarm. I like having my county calm and peaceful. I don't want that to change."

"No, I reckon not, I . . ."

"Excuse me, sir." A man with graying hair and a pencil-thin mustache had approached the table. "My apologies for intruding, but I wanted to ask you, Sheriff, if you've seen Adam today."

"No, I haven't, Larry. Is something wrong?"

"Oh, I wouldn't think so. It's just that he wasn't in for coffee this morning, and now he's gone and missed a committee meeting too. Missing meetings isn't like him at all and no one has heard anything from him."

"Damn!" Thompson blurted out. He dropped a coin onto the table and reached for his hat. "I hope there hasn't been. . . ." He did not finish the sentence.

Longarm said, "I'll go with you."

The two peace officers strode quickly outside and turned in the direction of Commissioner Terhune's house.

They found Terhune at home, still in his nightshirt and with a shawl wrapped around his shoulders.

"Dammit, I am sorry about that," Terhune said. "I haven't felt up to going out today, and the truth is that I forgot all about that meeting."

"There's no harm done," Thompson said. "I'll let everyone know. We were afraid something had happened to you."

"Only this sour belly. Why? Is there some reason in particular you were concerned today?"

"There's been an assault on Marshal Long here. For a moment there I was worried we were gonna find more of the same over here."

They told Terhune about the problems of last night and again this morning.

"You didn't ask," Terhune said, "but Martha was telling you the truth, Marshal. I was out at her place last night with most of the other large producers. We discussed . . . our options. Her man Gable was there. I don't think he ever left the room except maybe to take a piss. Certainly he couldn't have ridden into town and shot at you. I would swear to that if need be."

"No need for it," Longarm said. "I believe you. Believed her too. I don't know who or why, but it wasn't Gable that fired at me last night."

"It has to be whoever it is who is murdering us sheepmen," Terhune insisted. He belched and gave them a stricken look. " 'Scuse me."

The county commissioner turned and fled toward the privacy in the back of his home. They heard a door slam, and then the unmistakable splash and thunder of a man with the squirts.

"Poor sonuvabitch," Longarm said. "Must've eat something that didn't agree with him."

"He felt well enough last night to ride out to the Wesler place."

"That's a trip he wouldn't be wanting t' make today."

Terhune returned a few minutes later, bringing with him the dank and acid aroma of diarrhea. He looked like hell, his skin color more gray than pink, and there were dark half-moons under his eyes.

"I think . . . I think the murderer has killed me too," he said before sinking into his easy chair.

Chapter 32

"Why are we stopping in here?" Longarm asked.

"You said you want to talk with all the merchants who sell guns or ammunition, right? Well, Jake here sells some guns."

Longarm looked around with skepticism as they entered the cluttered farm supply store. There were hoes, spades, pruning saws, rakes, bone meal, fish meal, powdered lime . . . he didn't know what all else. He saw no sign of firearms or related items. But then he had told Thompson he wanted to speak with every merchant in town who might possibly have sold some .32 cartridges recently.

The proprietor was a heavyset man with a receding hairline and muttonchop side whiskers. Which, when Longarm thought about it, seemed a trifle out of place here on the fruit and farm side of town, although only because of the name.

The man, presumably the Jake that Bill Thompson mentioned, looked at Longarm with suspicious reserve. Probably the community had decided that the visiting federal officer had come to support the sheepmen, Longarm thought.

Thompson explained their purpose. The sheriff had

been the one to pose the questions at every store they'd visited. Both he and Longarm thought the locals might speak a little more freely to him than to a stranger.

Jake only shook his head. But then all the others had too. "I don't carry any pistol cartridges. Not unless you count .22 BB caps. I sell a few boxes of those each year. They're good for potting rats and like that. But really, all I offer are a few shotguns. A little loose powder and shot and percussion caps. Oh, and I do carry some of these war-surplus rifles." He pointed to a rack where five old wartime Springfield rifled muskets stood. The outmoded guns were muzzle-loaders when they left the Springfield Armory years back. Sometime afterward they had been changed over to use breech-loaded brass cartridges with the Allyn conversion system.

"I freighted in ten crates of these old things. The fellow I bought them from thought I was crazy to take so many, but those five are all I have left. I wish now I'd bought more. The good thing is that I bought plenty of ammunition for them. Those old guns are going to make this a pretty good month for me. I may just apply to one of those agencies back East that will fix you up with a mail-order bride." He nodded. "Get myself one of those red-headed Irish girls. I hear tell they work hard and have big, soft titties. I don't suppose you'd know if they got red hair down below same as on top?"

"It's red down below too," Longarm said, earning him a nod of appreciation from the storekeeper. "I take it you've only recently sold those muskets?"

"That's right."

"To farmers."

"Uh-huh."

Longarm did not like the sound of that. The sheepmen might have hired a gunman to take their side, but now it looked like the farmers were arming the whole damned county. "How many rifles to the crate?" he asked.

"Six."

Longarm frowned. Ten crates. Sixty rifles. And all but five of them recently sold. That was scary.

"Getting back to the .32's," Thompson said, either ignoring that point or missing it, "has anybody else asked you about cartridges for one of those guns lately?"

"That what was used to shoot at the marshal last night?" Jake asked.

"That's right."

"I'll tell you what I think," Jake said, "and that's that you fellows are barking up the wrong tree if you're looking for somebody to've bought shells lately. Let me show you something." He reached beneath his counter and set a cedar cigar box onto it. Inside the box he had several turnip-shaped key-wind watches, a few coins that looked foreign in origin, and a nickel-plated Ivor Johnson break-top .32 that was rusting in the places where the plating was cracked.

"I've had this gun since Methuselah was in diapers," Jake said, "and I've never bought a cartridge for it since the day I bought it. I bought a box then, and took the gun out to the shitter and fired one shot into the hole just to make sure the thing worked. Then I put it into this box, and haven't touched it since except to push it aside when I'm looking for something else. Come to think of it, I have no idea whatever happened to the rest of the cartridges in that original box. I haven't seen them in I can't remember how long. But I still have the five that are loaded in this cylinder.

"What I think is that if you were shot at by a gun like this, well, it really was a gun like this. A put-aside gun, not something to use or rely on. Just something that a man would have sitting around in a drawer in his bedroom bureau or on a shelf along with the hats he doesn't wear any longer."

Longarm grunted. But when they were outside again he

told Thompson, "The man's probably right, Bill. Looking for that gun is the proverbial needle in a haystack thing."

"Yeah, but if we don't look we certainly can't find."

"So. Can you think of anyplace else to look?"

The sheriff shook his head. "Jake was the last. But when you think about it, there are probably a couple dozen .32's and .38's and old-timey caplock pistols kicking around in sock drawers, pretty much forgotten about and certainly not out where anyone would see them or know they were there."

"What worries me more than that," Longarm said, "is the thought that there are dozens of Springfield muskets out there all of a sudden now."

Thompson did not say anything. And Longarm was reminded that Sheriff Bill Thompson was, after all, from a dirt-farming background himself.

"Reckon I'm gonna go have supper," Longarm said. "I don't know about you, but I've walked about all I can enjoy for one day."

"If you need me I'll be in the office until evening rounds at ten or so, then home after that."

Longarm told him good night and headed toward Hilda's Café.

Chapter 33

Longarm groaned. He felt like somebody was stabbing him in the gut with a red-hot branding iron. He needed to take a crap. Bad.

Fairly sure he didn't have time to make it to the backhouse before things started squirting, he grabbed the thunder mug from underneath the bed and squatted over it.

"Aw, shit!" The term in this case was more than merely literal. The explosion of stinking brown fluid hit the basin with such force that some of it splashed back onto him. He could feel it drip and run. The sensation was not exactly pleasing.

But at least the hurting in his gut eased. The branding iron went elsewhere.

He stayed there poised above the container until he was sure there was nothing more going to happen, then poured water into the washbasin so he could clean himself. By the time he was done with that he had to crap again. He half-filled the thunder mug before his bowels were finally empty and he could crawl weakly back into bed.

No wonder Terhune had looked so uncomfortable if this was what . . . dammit, this was the same problem, wasn't it. Both of them must have eaten something that very badly disagreed with them, although Longarm did not know what.

He would worry about that in the morning, though. This middle-of-the-night belly misery was cutting too deep into his beauty rest.

Longarm felt considerably better in the morning. Felt light on his feet for one thing, and so he should. After all, there wasn't anything left in any part of his digestive tract. That all went away the night before.

He took time to take the thunder mug out to the outhouse and empty it himself rather than make Miss Wannamacher clean it. Even with the lid on, the crockery lifesaver stank. He dumped it in the hole and had his morning piss, then got a pail of water from the backyard pump and rinsed the heavy crock before he took it back inside.

By then his landlady was already long gone, taking her biscuit dough with her, to prepare the café for the morning crowd. Longarm brushed his hair and decided he could get along without a shave at least until past noon, then made sure his Colt was riding loose in its holster before he stepped out onto the street.

Jedediah Gable was stretched out on a plank in the back room at the barbershop, but the fact remained: *Somedamn-body* had taken a shot at him the other night, and that somebody was not Jed Gable. Whoever it was, and why they'd done it, both the person and the reason could be presumed to have remained in the vicinity.

On an impulse—having mostly to do with the fact that he liked her little girl's smile—Longarm turned not toward Hilda Wannamacher's café, but to the one run by the pleasant lady named Maggie. He would have to pay to eat there, but what the hell. In the long run it would come out of Uncle Sam's pocket, not his. When he got back he would just mark it down on an expense reimbursement form, along along with everything else he'd spent before admitting to being a deputy marshal, and Henry would see to the details for him.

He was in luck. The kid was on duty at this hour. Smiling and cute as a button. She seemed pleased to see him. "Good morning, Marshal."

"Good morning, uh . . . do you know something awful? I don't know your name."

She giggled and blushed although he had no idea why. "I'm Sarah Anne Jones. There's an e on the end of Anne, but the Sarah part is plain and so is Jones."

"Nope," he said, "there's nothing plain about you. And I am delighted to properly make your acquaintance." He already had his hat off, but swept it low now as he bowed and made a leg before her.

That sent Sarah Anne into a fresh spate of giggling and blushing. This time she got so red her freckles almost disappeared. And it took a powerful lot of redness to do that.

The place was nearly full, but Longarm found a vacant seat at a table already occupied by two men in bib overalls and low-cut shoes. "Mind if I join you?" he asked.

"Help y'self."

After he sat, his table companions eyed him for a moment before either spoke. Then the one who was clean-shaven—the other had a spade beard—said, "You're that marshal fella, ain't you?"

"I am," Longarm agreed.

"Shouldn't you be over on t'other side of the crick?"

"Why?" he asked, deliberately misunderstanding.

"You're here t' help those sheepherding sons of bitches, ain't you?"

"I'm here to see the law is observed," Longarm told him. "For everybody. Including you."

Sarah Anne brought him a cup of fresh coffee and set it down. She must have overheard at least a little of the conversation because she gave a dirty look to the fellow who'd spoken and snapped, "Mr. Hankins, the marshal here is a friend of mine, and I want you to take back what you said or I'll . . . I'll . . . I'll tell Mama. And I'll put salt in your coffee. Just you see if I don't."

Hankins smiled and said, "If this man is a friend of yours, Sary Anne, then I take back everything I said an' then some."

"Well . . . all right then." She whirled around, her skirts flying, and with a loud sniff stamped away toward the kitchen.

She was back a moment later, looking sheepish and blushing some more. "I forgot to ask what you want for breakfast," she said to Longarm in a very small voice.

"Eggs if you have them. And a pork chop. Biscuits. A little gravy."

"Fried taters?"

"Sure, let's give it the works this morning."

She grinned and again darted away, chipper and happy this time.

"Nice kid," Longarm said.

"Yeah, well, if Sary Anne likes you, I expect you can't be so bad, mister. My name is Tom. My friend here is George."

"My pleasure, gents."

One thing Longarm had to say. The coffee here was damn sure better than Hilda Wannamacher's.

And the waitress was sure cuter too.

The farmer was right on that score. Sarah Anne was a charmer, and that's all there was to it.

Chapter 34

"You look like hell this morning," the sheriff said by way of a greeting.

"That's reasonabie," Longarm told him. "I feel like hell. Well, I did during the night anyhow. Not so bad now that I have something in my stomach again. I was up half the night with the runs."

"I hope there's not an epizootic going around. First the commissioner. Now you. I know how to stand up to a man, but what do you do about a sickness?"

"Wait for it t' go away is about all I've ever known t' do," Longarm said. "I expect this is just something I ate that don't agree with me. Prob'ly it's the same with Terhune."

"He wasn't at the café this morning," Thompson said. "But then neither were you, I noticed."

"I like the coffee better at Maggie's." Longarm smiled and admitted, "Like the company better there too."

"You got something going with Maggie Jones?"

Longarm laughed. "No, but I'm sure crazy about that little girl of hers. I like that kid. Better coffee there too."

"Really? I've always liked Hilda's coffee." Thompson shrugged. "Not that it matters. Any plans for today?"

"Not really. I want to make a show of moving around. First to make the sheep crowd think I'm taking Terhune's murder charges serious enough to investigate them. Window dressing like that is really all I was sent over here for. And the second thing is that I want to see if anybody shows any guilty interest or maybe takes another shot at me. I'd still like t' find the sonuvabitch who did that. Otherwise, I'd be pulling out and heading back to Denver today or tomorrow at the latest."

"Is there anything I can do to help?"

Longarm shook his head. "Nothing I can think of, Bill, but thank you for the offer. I'll just prowl around some and make a nuisance of myself. Sometimes that's about all a fellow can do."

"Let me know if you change your mind."

"Will do, thanks." Longarm left the courthouse and paused outside to light a cheroot. He thought about walking across the street to put in an appearance at Hilda Wannamacher's café, but decided against it. He still had the taste of that good breakfast at Maggie's in his mouth. And the coffee at Hilda's would take that away from him. He took his time putting a just-right coal on the tip of his smoke, then tossed the spent match aside and began walking in the direction of Commissioner Terhune's house. If he was going to oversee the mending of political fences for the governor, it couldn't hurt to stop by this morning and inquire as to the commissioner's health.

Commissioner Terhune's housekeeper, Regina, answered Longarm's knock. She said nothing, just stood there looking expectantly up at him. Small as she was, she had a considerable distance to bridge.

Longarm removed his hat. "I'd like to see the commissioner please, ma'am."

She nodded and took a step backward, holding the door for him and pointing toward the study where the commissioner liked to do his business. Longarm helped himself to the same chair he'd occupied before, and sat waiting.

He heard Regina's footsteps clatter rather loudly up the stairs. Apparently Terhune was not yet up and around for the day. Not all that surprising, Longarm thought, if the man was still sick. A couple of solid days like his own past night and Longarm probably wouldn't want to get up and face the world either.

He heard the creak of floorboards overhead.

And then a shrill, terrified scream.

Longarm bolted from the comfort of the chair and raced up the staircase with his Colt in hand.

Chapter 35

It wasn't something worth all that screeching hysteria. At least not the way Longarm saw it. The man was dead, sure, but it wasn't like it was a bloody, violent sort of death. He hadn't been murdered or anything like that. He'd just . . . died.

Hart County commissioner Adam Terhune lay tucked snug beneath the covers of his own bed, stretched out as if asleep. Damned long sleep. This sleep he would not wake from.

His skin was pale, with a yellowish and somewhat waxy appearance, making his unshaven whiskers seem exceptionally dark and prominent. His hair was tousled and sort of plastered down in spots, suggesting he'd been sweating heavily just before he died, while the blanket pulled high indicated he'd been cold at the same time.

But then there was no question that he'd been sick. Obviously, there was much more than a simple case of the trots that had been knotting his belly.

Longarm took a moment to fret about his own body sensations. After all, he'd just spent a night with the squirts himself.

Fortunately, as far as he could see, the comparisons

stopped there. He wasn't feeling especially cold or weak or otherwise sick. He'd just had the runs. And as far as he could tell now, that seemed to have gone away. His breakfast lay warm and pleasant in his belly, and he was not sweating or shaky. His strength seemed perfectly normal. Wasn't it?

He frowned. A man could worry himself into believing almost anything if he thought about it hard enough. Including his own illness. Hell, as a kid Longarm—that was a nickname he couldn't even have imagined then, but Custis translated pretty easily into Cuss back then—little Cuss Long had been able to convince himself that he had a bellyache and oughtn't make the walk to the schoolhouse just about any time he had something more important to do. Best to stop imagining foolishness now and pay attention to business.

Not that there was any of his sort of business that needed taking care of here and now. Adam Terhune would surely have been bleating about murder most foul had he been alive to do so. As it was, well, there was nothing in this room to suggest that the gentleman's demise was anything but an illness gone a step too far for recovery.

Just to make sure no one questioned his judgment afterward, Longarm made a point to examine the inside of the second-floor window. The window itself was open, but there was one of those wire-mesh screen things put over the opening to keep flies and such from coming in, and that was secured with hooks and eyes. No intruder had crept in during the night to murder Terhune in his bed.

Longarm pulled the sheet back and gave the dead man a looking over. He had no marks on him to suggest he'd been strangled or smothered or such. And there was no blood. No stab or bullet wounds. No indications of any form of violence.

He hadn't been dead very long. Not long enough for all the blood to pool in the low spots. Not that Longarm supposed it mattered exactly when the commissioner died. The point was that he'd had a mighty good reason to miss having coffee with his pals this morning.

And come to think of it, not only would that table be short one member from now on, so would the Hart County commission.

Longarm wasn't sure how a thing like this would be handled, but if he remembered correctly, the governor would appoint a replacement to fill Terhune's seat until an election would make the change permanent.

My, wasn't that going to be interesting. Would the governor's people decide to throw in with the farmers now that the sheep faction was in a voting minority in Hart County? Or would the current state administration stick with their old friends and keep a sheep majority on the commission for the time being?

Longarm suspected he knew how that would go. If the dirt farmers were the wave of the future here, he'd bet the gov'ner was going to be making new friends and forging fresh alliances over here and damn quick about it.

Not, thank goodness, that was anything a grown-up Cuss Long had to fret over.

But he did think there was one step he ought to take in the interest of peace and tranquility.

He excused himself from the grieving housekeeper, stopped by the sheriff's office—Thompson was not in, so Longarm left a note informing him—and then headed for the livery to reclaim his horse and saddle.

"My apologies for intruding, ma'am, but I thought you should be the first to know," Longarm told the matriarch of the sheep clans. "I know you were close to him."

Martha Wesler snorted. "Adam was an idiot, Marshal. He thought there were ghosts in every closet and goblins beneath every bed. But he was *my* idiot, and I shall miss him."

"Yes, ma'am."

"The problem now . . . I thought we had more time to prepare," she said. "Now . . ."

"That's what I came out here t' mention to you, ma'am. Other than the obvious, that is. The way I understand things, there's now a fifty-fifty split on the county commission, so neither sheep nor farm can claim a majority. The governor bein' the sort of staunch and steadfast fella that he is"—that drew another snort of derision from the lady—"you can't count on him comin' to your rescue."

"Hardly," she agreed. "That sniveling weasel will trim his sails to whatever direction the wind is blowing, and we all know it."

"Yes'm, and the breeze seems t' be comin' from a new direction all of a sudden here."

"I fear so, young man." She peered intently at him for a moment. "What is your interest in this?"

"Same as I've told you before. Peace. I'm a peace officer. It's a term as means something to me. I know you've been planning t' disrupt the completion of that irrigation ditch. An' you needn't deny it."

"I don't believe I said a word there, Marshal. I'm content to listen. For the time being, at any rate. What I choose to do afterward is none of your business."

"Yes'm, and if it stays none o' my business I will be mighty happy. Because if it becomes my business, the first thing I'll do is go for the top. You cut the head off most any snake an' it isn't so scary anymore."

"You would put a harmless old woman in jail, Marshal?"

"Now, ma'am, we aren't talkin' about women here nor jail. We're talking about controlling varmints, whatever shape they come in. But yes, if need be, I'd do whatever the law and good sense require. So what I'm asking you, ma'am, is to be real careful when you reevaluate your situation here. You no longer have a local government majority you can count on. Truth is, you no longer have support you can count on from the state government neither. You no longer have a gunslinger . . . not that you had a very good one t' begin with . . . that you can turn to. An' you have a deputy United States marshal peering over your shoulder, and ma'am, I'm beholden to no one on any side of this. I don't do favors any more than I take them. D'you understand what I'm saying, ma'am?"

"You are very blunt."

"Yes, ma'am. Rude too sometimes. But I'm not intending any surprises here. Just hoping t' keep the peace. There's never a good time for a range war. But if there was such a thing, well, it's done run out on you now. The time is over. You missed it."

"What is it that you are telling me to do?"

"I wouldn't presume t' *tell* you a dang thing, ma'am. I got no authority t' do that. But what I am *suggesting* is that you sheep folks and your farm and fruit-growing neighbors work out an accommodation. They build their irrigation system without interference. Hell . . . excuse me . . ."

"I've heard worse. No need to apologize."

"Yes, ma'am. Thank you. Anyway, what I just happened t' think of was that maybe you could actually help them route their ditch. Build it on both sides o' the stream, not just the one like it is now. An' plan it out so it waters fenced farm or orchard land in one spot an' improved pasture in the next. Could work out t' give you folks better graze than this scrub you're grazing now. With all the land you folks control, how many sheep could you carry on it if it was irrigated an' green instead of being mostly sagebrush an' soapweed?"

Mrs. Wesler blinked. Her shoulders straightened and she sat more fully upright in her chair.

She did not respond. But Longarm knew that thought had grabbed her attention. Hard. The thought of putting her sheep on improved pasture was an attractive one. And with a little cooperation between the sheep and the farm factions . . . why the hell not? It could happen. If both parties wanted it to.

"That's all I came t' say, ma'am. If you'll excuse me now, I reckon I'd best head back t' town."

"You will stay for lunch, I hope."

"No, ma'am, I can't, although I thank you for the offer. Duty calls, y'know."

She raised an eyebrow, but did not question him. "Very well."

"G'bye, ma'am." Longarm picked up his Stetson and headed for the door. Before he got there she stopped him.

"Marshal."

"Yes, ma'am?"

"Thank you. Thank you very much."

He smiled at her. "Yes, ma'am. My pleasure."

With any sort of luck, he thought as he went outside and headed for his horse, there would be no more gunmen hired by the sheep folks here, no ditch blocking or spillway breaking. No range war at all.

With luck and common sense.

There were no guarantees about it, of course. But a person could hope.

Hope is good.

He untied the horse and stepped lightly into his saddle.

It wasn't exactly duty that was calling him now. But something damn sure was.

Chapter 36

Dammit anyway! Sissy Beckham was not alone when Longarm got there. She and a tall, gangly gent were standing beside the pump in her front yard. A buckboard with a pair of very small, shaggy ponies was parked nearby.

"G'day, miss," Longarm said, touching the brim of his Stetson. "And g'morning to you, sir." He glanced overhead toward the sun, partially hidden behind a puffball of cloud. "Or afternoon, whichever it might be."

"Hello, Marshal. Step down, please. Have you met James?"

"I haven't had the pleasure yet," Longarm said as he dismounted and extended his hand.

"James Wick, Custis Long." She smiled at the lanky farmer. "Mr. Long is the deputy United States marshal. I'm sure you've heard about him."

"Yes, of course. Pleased to meet you, Marshal." He did not sound particularly pleased, but he was nice enough to offer the words anyway.

"My pleasure, I'm sure," Longarm said with equal enthusiasm.

"James is my neighbor to the south one farm over."

"I see," Longarm said, not knowing what the hell else

he could say. Nice dirt around here? Get much rain, do you? The few things that might come to mind were not exactly of riveting interest. Not to him anyway. He hadn't liked farming worth a shit when he was a kid, and hadn't found any reason to improve his view of it since—a farmer's view being mostly that of a mule's skinny ass.

He could tell that Wick was having the same sort of awkwardness. But then what would a dirt farmer say to a lawman? Shoot any felons this morning, Marshal? Like putting people in jail do you, Deputy?

"James came by to return some pruning shears he took to sharpen for me," Sissy put in. She, unlike the men, seemed quite content with the moment. "And now that you are here, Custis, we can all have lunch without my reputation being compromised." Longarm could see a twinkle in her eye.

"You will stay to eat, won't you, Custis?"

"I don't want t' put you out, miss, an' I never thought t' pack any grub along t' help out."

"Oh, don't give that a thought. I have plenty. I set a plain table but a bountiful one." She smiled. "It is one of the advantages of raising one's own food, you see. We may have little in the way of worldly possessions, but we eat very well. Isn't that right, James?"

Wick dropped his gaze and scuffed his shoe in the dirt. He mumbled something that sounded like he was agreeing with her.

"Come inside now. Both of you."

"You're very kind," Longarm said. "Mind if I water my horse and pull the saddle first? It'll do him good t' let the air an' sunshine reach his back for a bit."

"Go right ahead then."

Longarm led the bay gelding into the pen where Sissy's horse was kept. He let it drink, but but did not fork any hay from the rick into the feed bunk. Hay would be hard to come by out here, and the horse was getting everything it needed at the livery in town.

Behind him he saw a frowning James Wick lean close to Sissy and say something. She shook her head and laid her fingertips on the farmer's forearm, but he would not be dissuaded from whatever it was he'd just told her. A moment later Wick climbed onto the driving seat of his buckboard and took up the lines, spanking his ponies into a quick-footed, head-bobbing trot. He pulled out of the yard in the direction of the unfinished irrigation ditch and Weirville.

"I didn't mean t' run anybody off," Longarm apologized when he joined Sissy beside the pump, where she was finishing the chore of drawing a bucket of cool water. Longarm waited until she was done, then lifted the bucket from the iron spout.

"You did me a favor really. James is a dear, dear man. And quite infatuated with me if I do immodestly say so. I believe he would propose marriage if I encouraged him. But as nice as he is, I can imagine very little that would be more dreary and boring than to be married to him. And I very much doubt that he would be able to scratch my itches. Certainly not the way you do."

Longarm grinned. "I can't blame him for bein' smitten with you." He shifted the bucket of water to his other hand and wrapped an arm around Sissy's waist. "There's a lot o' woman inside that skinny body o' yours."

"Do you really think so?"

"Lady, it wasn't the thought o' lunch that brought me out here this afternoon. I was kinda hoping to scratch those itches you mentioned."

Sissy laughed. "Good."

She led the way inside, and Longarm set the water bucket beside the stove. "D'you want me t' fill the reservoir for you?"

"Later," she said. She raised her arms in that deliberately provocative way women have—he'd seen a hundred of them do it, and they all used the same slow, sexy, two-handed motion that straightened their necks and lifted their tits for display—and began unfastening the pins that held her hair in place. "Right now there is something else I'd like for you to do."

Chapter 37

"Something else" turned out to be interesting indeed. Enjoyable too.

Sissy disrobed completely, standing naked in the broad noonday light for Longarm to admire all he wished.

She was so lean her ribs were prominent, as were the sharp bones of her pelvis. Plump women are comfortable to lie on, but Longarm found a certain attraction too in the skinny ones whose bones were so easily felt pressing into a man's flesh when he pounded into her.

The woman was not fragile, though, as he had reason to remember. She was as tough and resilient as a bullhide whip. Pretty much the same thickness too.

She laughed, turning to let him see all he wished, then came to him on tiptoes to place a slow, lingering kiss on his mouth while her fingers sought the buttons and buckles of his clothing.

"I want to see your body," she said. "I want to see you naked."

Longarm had no objection. His only answer was to cup her chin in one hand and a breast in the other while he kissed her. Today she tasted of mint. Nice.

In less than a minute he too was naked. Outside, a

breeze sprang up, reaching in through the open doorway and windows to play across their flesh. Longarm enjoyed the feel of it. Enjoyed the feel of Sissy's skin even more as he held her to him and ran his hands over her back and down onto her butt.

"Wait. Let me see." She pulled away from him, ducking underneath his embrace, and stood back to admire Longarm's muscular body. "Do you know who Adonis was?"

"Some dead Greek guy, right?"

She laughed. "A Greek god. The very ideal of masculine beauty. You could pose for a statue of him." She laughed again. "Well, except for your face. You are all craggy and handsome, but all the drawings and statues of Adonis show him as being almost pretty, with curly hair and pouty lips. I think you are ever so much more handsome than that kind of man."

Her eyes drifted south. "The statues always show Adonis naked, you know. So I can tell you with some authority that you're also hung better."

It was Longarm's turn to laugh. He reached out and pulled her to him again. She came quite willingly.

"Damn, you taste good," he said a minute or two later. He bent, slipped an arm behind her knees, and picked her up, carrying her to the bed and placing her gently down there. Sissy smiled.

"I want to taste your juice," she said. "I want you to come in my mouth the first time. I want to take the essence of you into my body. I want to consume it and make you a part of me." She winked. "I also want to use up all that nice stuff where it can't knock me up."

Longarm laughed again. He did like this girl. Damned if he didn't. "Tell you what. You want a taste o' me. How about if I do the same for you?"

"You wouldn't!"

"Hell, yes, I will. Though I haven't shaved yet today. I'll try an' be careful."

Sissy shivered. "I don't care. If you . . . I've always wanted to feel that. I've never known a man who didn't think . . . never mind. Yes. Oh, yes. Please."

"Roll over," Longarm told her.

"But . . ."

"No, just do it. I know what I'm up to."

"All right. Whatever you say."

"Now that's an attitude that I can like."

Sissy turned over onto her stomach. "You aren't going to take me back there, are you?"

"No, I'm not going to do that."

"Then what . . ."

"Hush. Just close your eyes and relax."

He lifted the spill of red hair that lay spread over her back and placed it on the pillow so that it covered her face and eyes. She would not need to see in order to enjoy this.

Slowly, patiently, starting at the nape of her neck, Longarm began to lick and nibble at Sissy Beckham's pale and lovely flesh.

She shivered and squirmed. She moaned and cried out. Twice he was fairly sure she climaxed as he moved downward, covering every inch of her skin with the ministrations of his tongue.

She giggled when he licked her side just above the hipbone. Ticklish there, he thought. But instead of ignoring the area, he made sure his contact was firmer there, harder and more deliberate so it would tantalize but not tickle.

He ran his tongue into the crack of her ass, then made sure to look and sniff to make sure she was completely clean before he went any further.

He licked and nuzzled the backs of her legs, paying particular attention to the sensitive flesh behind her knees. Then swiftly lower to the soles of her feet. Between her toes. Back upward.

"On your back now."

This time there was neither question nor hesitation. Sissy rolled over and let her legs move slightly apart for him.

He worked his way up onto her thighs, then skipped to her head. Licked her face. Her ears. Brought a yelp of surprise and shock from her when he playfully stuck his tongue into one nostril.

Longarm chuckled and made up for it by kissing her. She shuddered, and he was fairly sure she'd come again.

He lingered long on her nipples. Explored her armpits. Made her writhe when he licked her navel.

And finally . . .

She was sopping wet, small droplets of slippery fluid clinging to the bright red pussy hair even before he contributed his saliva.

She cried out when his tongue found the tiny button of pleasure that stood proud at the entrance to her. She shuddered violently and grabbed the back of his head.

After another few minutes Longarm rocked back onto his heels and smiled at her. "Now," he said, "I reckon it's your turn t' give me a bath."

"Yes, dear. Yes. Please!"

A person would be hard-pressed to think of a nicer way to spend an afternoon, he idly thought a few minutes later as Sissy gleefully repaid the pleasure.

Chapter 38

"If you ever need a testimonial," Longarm said, idly stirring sugar into his coffee, "I'd be glad t' tell the world that you are a mighty fine fuck, Miss Beckham."

She roared. "Thank you. I think. But let's leave the world in doubt on that subject, shall we?"

"Just makin' the offer, that's all."

"You're a gentleman to the core," she told him.

"Maybe, but a hungry one." They never had gotten around to that lunch she'd promised. Now it was too late for that. Supper would just have to do instead.

"They'll be ready in a minute." She was making flapjacks.

Longarm poured a dollop of canned milk into his cup, stirred again, and took a hearty mouthful. "Jeez!" Coffee sprayed across the table and onto the floor as, gagging, he spewed it out.

"What happened? Are you all right?"

"I think . . . there's salt in this coffee, not sugar. Damn!" He took up the offending jar and sniffed, then placed a pinch of the crystals on the palm of his hand and touched the tip of his tongue to them. "Uh-huh. Salt."

"Oh, dear. I am *so* sorry. I must have gotten the wrong

jar by mistake." She took that one and whisked it away, replacing it a moment later with a similar jar containing very similar white crystals.

This time Longarm wet a fingertip and dunked it into the stuff to taste before using. This time it was sugar, all right.

By that time Sissy had tossed the ruined coffee outside. She refilled his cup and set it in front of him, planting a kiss on him while she was in the vicinity. "I'm sorry, dear." Then she laughed again. "But just think. It could have been worse. I might have grabbed the rat poison instead."

He made a face. "Thank goodness for small favors, eh?"

"Ooo!" She raced to the stove and snatched up the heavy griddle, sliding the first pancakes off onto a plate. "Don't turn them over. They may be burned. But if you don't see, you'll never know, right?"

"Your logic could be better," he told her.

"You don't have to eat those if you don't want them. I'll have more ready in another few minutes."

"Hush up, woman, an' hand me that jar o' honey. But be careful. I'd hate t' put axle grease on these flapjacks by mistake."

Longarm scratched Sissy's itch one more time after supper, but declined her suggestion that he stay the night. "You tempt me, but I reckon not," he said. "I got work t' do. Besides, think o' your reputation. Farmer Jones might see my horse here t'morra and come to the logical conclusions."

"His name is Wick, as you remember perfectly well, and it might not be an entirely bad thing for him to know I'm an evil woman. It might make him stop making calves' eyes at me."

"Might make him start talking about you t' the neighbors too," Longarm reminded her. "No, best thing will be for me t' head back to town now. There's still things I need t' do there."

But there were things he still wanted to do at Sissy Beckham's farm too. It was late in the evening by the time Longarm reached the livery stable. He had no idea where the hostler was, so he unsaddled and put the horse up himself, scooping a healthy measure of grain into the trough and forking fresh hay into the bunk as well. He was paying for this feed, and so felt no reluctance about using as he had back at Sissy's.

Finally, yawning hugely, he trudged out of the barn and turned toward Miss Wannamacher's house on the other side of the creek.

He was in the middle of the connecting bridge when a burst of light and noise sounded from somewhere to his right, and he heard the zipping bee-drone sound of a bullet passing close by his face.

Chapter 39

Longarm wound up on his hands and knees in the icy water of the creek, Colt in hand but with no target visible on the other side of the bridge.

He was already so wet, a little more wouldn't hurt. He crouched even lower and eased beneath the bridge and through to the other side.

A thin screen of brush lined the banks on the upstream side of the bridge, the direction from which the shot had come. Presumably the shot was fired from there. The question now was, was the gunman still there, waiting for another chance, or had he once again slipped away without waiting to determine the outcome of his ambush?

Son of a *bitch*, Longarm silently grumbled.

He was commencing to shiver like an aspen leaf in a high wind. The damn water seemed to get colder the longer he was in it.

He moved silently to his left, toward the farm-side bank, where he'd been headed before this interruption, and stood. When the night air reached him through his wet clothing, he felt colder than ever.

Fuck this! He was not going to stand there and having escaped a bullet, die of pneumonia instead. He waded out of the water and moved along the bank in the direction of where the gunman had been when he fired.

There was . . . nothing. The son of a bitch was gone. Again.

Thoroughly pissed off, Longarm angrily shoved the Colt back into his holster and waddled, legs wide apart and boots half-full of cold water, the rest of the way to Miss Wannamacher's house.

She was still up, he saw, or anyway had left a light burning for him. He dripped his way onto the porch and let himself in.

"Stop!"

He stopped.

"What did you do? Get drunk and fall in the water? It will serve you right if you catch your death of cold. No, don't come another step, not until I bring a towel." She sniffed. "Several towels, I should think."

The spinster whirled about and disappeared into the back of the house. She was back a minute later with a stack of flour-sack towels, most of which she handed to him. The rest she used herself, her concern being for the floor and not the boarder. Not that he could fault her for that actually.

"You don't reek of liquor," she said accusingly once the floor had been dried and he was standing over another towel so it could catch the water that continued to drip—more slowly now—from him. "How did a sober man manage to get this wet? Did you get into a brawl and someone threw you in? Humph! Men! Indeed."

Longarm couldn't help proclaiming his innocence. He explained, although without elaborate detail.

Miss Wannamacher's eyes became wide. "Shot at you? Oh, no. Just like the assassination attempt at Harry Sprague's home a few nights ago. Oh, dear. Nothing . . . nothing like this has *ever* happened in Weirville. Never.

Not from the very first days. Oh, my. Do you know who did it? Do you have any suspects?"

"No'm, I don't," Longarm admitted.

"Oh, you poor man. I want you to go change into something dry and come into the kitchen. You're shivering, you poor thing. I was just making a pot of tea for myself. I like to have a cup to unwind after all day at the restaurant, but I can make coffee instead. Would you rather have coffee? I thought so. Now you go on. Get yourself dry and comfortable. I'll have coffee for you when you come back. I'll be in the kitchen. Go on now. Hurry up before you catch your death."

It really would be a bitch to die from getting wet after all the times he'd been shot at, Longarm thought wryly as he duck-waddled—damn, but it felt horrible to walk in wet britches—on to his room to dry off and change clothes.

Nothing but time and the dry, high desert air was going to help his boots, but once he'd dried himself, he used the dirty towels to swab them out as best he could, then hung them upside down on the bedposts so the air could get into them.

Fortunately he did have a change of clothing available, although it was only his rough traveling gear. That would just have to do and never mind the town duds.

He dressed, then walked barefoot save for his socks back to Hilda Wannamacher's kitchen.

She was as good as her word. The coffee was hot and ready, already laced thick with canned milk and heaps of brown sugar. She was stirring it into a cup for him when he arrived, her expression intent as she tried to get it just the way he liked it.

"This is good, miss. Thank you." He'd almost made the mistake of calling her "ma'am." It was a common enough problem with spinster ladies. They weren't married and likely never would be, but their age and appearance made it almost an automatic thing to speak to and about them as if they were in the "madam" instead of "miss" category.

"It is the very least I can do," she said. "Now sit there and relax. I have some pie left over from today. I put it into the oven to warm up for you."

"You're very kind."

She only sniffed. And went to the oven to see if the pie was warm enough to satisfy her.

It was. And Longarm felt considerably better once he had pie and coffee warming him from the inside out.

Chapter 40

He woke up biting back an impulse to scream. The pain. The pain. He clutched his belly with both hands and gasped. It felt like fire. Knives. Burning knives. Stabbing. Stabbing. Over and over.

His gut churned, and the acid burned his butt.

He fumbled his way off the bed, falling off it more than getting off it.

He grabbed the thunder mug and squatted over it. That brought some measure of relief. But his belly. That was still afire.

He turned, on hands and knees, and puked into the thunder mug, adding that to the already stinking contents of the container.

He burned at both ends, and worst of all in the middle.

His butt was sore and stinging from the acid in his loose, watery crap, and his mouth was foul with the vile flavor of vomit.

He felt like he was going to die.

He did *not* feel like he wanted to die.

He crawled, barely able to manage that, to the washstand beside the bedroom window, and grabbed the pitcher of fresh water waiting there to wash with in the morning. Instead he lifted it down, his hands shaking and body atremble, and drank from it.

He drank all he could hold, then crawled back to the thunder mug and tried to puke again. He couldn't, so he ran a finger into his own throat until he gagged and was able to throw up again.

Yellowish brown water spewed out of his mouth, overflowing the thunder mug onto the floor. Fuck it. What were rugs for if not to sop up puke?

He turned and crawled to the washstand again. This time he was a little steadier, a little stronger when he picked up the pitcher and drank down everything that remained in it.

Again he forced himself to throw up. There was no point in going back to the thunder mug beside the bed. It was already full and then some. Instead he dragged the washbasin off the stand and puked into that. This time the vomit was almost clear. A little stringy with mucus, but with only the faintest hint of yellow to it.

Longarm pulled back away from the washstand. He hadn't strength enough to return to the bed. He was sure of that.

He lay down where he was, closed his eyes, and dropped into an exhausted sleep.

He was shaky when he woke. But he was alive. He managed to get to his feet and pull on his trousers and shirt, but the boots were too much for him. They were still damp inside, and he did not have strength enough to force his feet in while the wet leather clung to his flesh. The hell with it. Hell with the tweed coat and vest and tie too. But he buckled the gunbelt in place and made sure his Colt was loaded and ready.

It was not quite daylight when he walked, wobbly and halting, out onto the street and turned toward the business district several blocks away.

Miss Wannamacher must already have left for the café because the house Longarm left behind him was dark and silent.

He headed not toward Hilda's restaurant, but to the café where the little girl Sarah Anne waited tables offering smiles and dimples with the food.

Longarm got there . . . and collapsed at the front door.

"Mama. Mama! Come quick."

Longarm was barely aware of someone bending over him. Hell, he was barely aware that he'd fallen to begin with.

"Marshal? Whatever has happened? Have you been shot?"

He had to concentrate hard to focus his attention. The little girl was there. And her mother. It took him a moment to remember the mother's name. Maggie, that was it.

"And your feet. You're bleeding. You've cut your feet up walking."

He hadn't known that. They didn't hurt.

"Here. Try to help us. We'll get you inside." Between them, the woman and girl managed to half-lift and half-drag him into the café. They set him onto a chair.

"What happened, Marshal? Can we bring you something? Coffee perhaps?"

The thought of coffee made him gag. Not that there was anything left in his stomach to bring up. But that did not stop him from trying.

"Something . . . ate something. Bad," he said. "Need some . . . ipecac."

"You've already thrown up. I can smell it on your breath. I don't think you need ipecac now. Wait here."

Sarah Anne steadied him on the chair while her mother dashed away into her kitchen. She was back a few moments later with a small box with the sort of design on it that generally indicated a patent medicine was contained inside.

"What . . ."

"It's nothing but powdered charcoal," she said.

Longarm made a face.

"No, really. It will absorb any poisons still in your system." She smiled. "Trust me."

She dipped a teaspoonful out and fed it to him. The stuff tasted like shit—well, like powdered charcoal anyway—and he almost said so. Would have except for the presence of the little girl.

"Tastes terrible, doesn't it?" Sarah Anne put in.

Longarm nodded.

"We'll give the charcoal a few minutes to work. Then I want you to eat a little. Bread will be the best thing. I'll make you some milk toast." He must have shown what he thought about that because she said, "I'm not interested in what you like or what you want. My concern is what will be good for you."

"Yes, ma'am," he said meekly.

"Sarah dear, go slice some bread and set it on the toast rack. And warm some milk, please."

"Yes, Mama." The child hurried away on her mission of mercy.

Longarm watched her go, then said to her mother, "She's a good kid, isn't she?"

"She is my life."

"I can think o' worse causes."

"In case you are wondering, Marshal, you will be fine. You may need a little time to get your strength back, and it will take a while for those rock cuts on your feet to heal. But you are going to be fine."

"Y'know, I kinda came t' that conclusion my own self. But I have t' say, it's a fact that is gonna make somebody real, real mad."

"You can't mean . . . this couldn't have been deliberate."

"Oh, yes. I was poisoned. Twice. An' so, I think, was a bunch o' other fellas around here. You know that crazy county commissioner Terhune? I think wild as his story was, he was tellin' the truth. There really was a bunch o' murders here. The only genuinely crazy part of it wasn't his claim, but that fact that nobody knew about it. Not even the fellas that was murdered." Longarm shook his head.

"Would you like me to go get Sheriff Thompson?"

"Yes, thank you. I think that would be a really good idea, ma'am."

Chapter 41

Thompson borrowed a surrey to drive Longarm the several blocks back to Miss Wannamacher's so he could get his boots. By then Longarm was feeling well enough to dig around in his bag for a pair of clean socks, and with them on was able this time to get into his boots without more than just a little help from the Hart County sheriff.

"I can do this alone, you know," Thompson said for probably the twentieth time.

"I know you could, Bill, and I know you'd do a fine job of it, but this is a pleasure I want for myself if you don't mind."

"Lord knows you're entitled. You're also weak as a damn kitten and look like you'll fall over sideways if a breeze comes up."

"Be that as it may, I can still stand on my own hind legs. I'll do it." Longarm grinned. "But I'd appreciate it if you'd kinda stand there beside me just in case you got to reach out an' grab something to keep me from takin' that fall."

"I'll be there."

"Right. Now let's head for the courthouse, shall we?"

They got back into the surrey, Longarm with a boost

from Thompson, and the sheriff took up the driving lines and spanked the team into motion.

They stopped beside the courthouse, and Longarm managed to climb down to the ground without help. He kept a firm hold on the side rail, though, lest he end up wallowing in the dirt in case his legs buckled. He was still shaky. But upright, dammit. He was indeed standing on his own feet. He intended to stay that way.

With Thompson shadowing him by his elbow, Longarm crossed the street and pushed open the door to Hilda Wannamacher's café.

The lady was just coming out of the kitchen with a tray of heavily loaded breakfast platters.

She took one look at Longarm and dropped the tray. The crockery plates landed with a crash, food and splinters of shattered tableware flying in all directions.

"Surprised?" Longarm said mildly. "Thought I was dead in my bed, did you? Not that I'm sorry t' disappoint you, mind, but this time it didn't work. I guess whatever stuff you been using works better when you feed it a little at a time an' let it build up inside a man's system.

"That is the way you did it, isn't it? The men all came here every morning for breakfast, so it was easy as hell for you to do."

"I don't know what . . ."

"Of course you do. You, mister, in the corner, I don't know what you're thinking right now an' it could well be that you're only wanting t' scratch your belly, but friend, if you touch the butt o' that hogleg on your hip, I'll shoot you dead as the men this woman's killed."

"Easy, Charlie," Thompson put in. "The marshal knows what he's doing, so all of you calm down now and leave be. Better yet, I think every one of you needs to clear out of here. There won't be any more meals served. Not today and probably not for twenty or thirty years. So go on. All of you. Get out."

The locals didn't like it. But however reluctantly, they did comply. Thompson herded them around to the side and behind so no one passed between Longarm and Hilda Wannamacher, who continued to stand in the kitchen doorway.

"The way you move those boys where you want 'em, Bill, I got to say I think you'd make a pretty good sheepman," Longarm said. He cut his eyes toward Thompson for a fraction of a second. When he looked back, Miss Wannamacher had her hand in her apron pocket.

"What'd you use? Rat poison?"

"That's right."

"That why your coffee was bitter?"

"Was it? I never tasted it myself. I think you will understand why."

"No denials?"

"Why should I? I know you will look. You will find the poison. You already know what happened."

"Yes'm, but I still don't understand why," Longarm said.

"Don't you? Don't you, you son of a bitch? No, of course you don't. A man, a handsome man at that, could have no idea what it is like for a homely woman to find her one true love and then have it taken from her. Taken?" She snorted. "Stolen is more like it. Carl was in love with me. Can you believe that?"

"Who the hell is Carl?"

"Carl Wesler, of course. He loved me. He would have married me."

"My God, Hilda, Carl Wesler fucked every female between here and Virginia City. Either Virginia City, Nevada, or Montana. He didn't love anybody but himself," Bill Thompson put in.

"He did. He loved me. We were going to be married. He got down on his knee and asked me to marry him. Then . . . then those cowards made him leave. But he would have come back for me. I know he would have. Except he was murdered before he could return to get me. And once he was dead, when I knew there was no hope left for me . . . I knew I had to get back at those awful old men for ruining my life and my Carl's."

"So you killed them," Longarm said.

"So I killed them, yes. And I am proud of it."

"Fine. You can spend the rest of your life thinking how proud of yourself you are," he told her.

"I don't think I care to be imprisoned," she said with her chin high and her eyes unnaturally bright.

"Unfortunately, they won't hang you. Sorry. But they don't hang women. It isn't a choice they'll give you."

Her answer was to bring her hand out of the apron pocket. She took careful aim at Longarm with a small, break-top .32 revolver.

"Don't do it," he warned her.

She eared back the hammer.

"Dammit to hell anyway."

Longarm's big Colt thundered, the sound unnaturally loud inside the close confinement of four walls.

The slug took Hilda low in the belly, doubling her over and dropping her to her knees. The .32 fell from her grasp. It hit the floor muzzle down, the impact causing the hammer to drop. The little weapon fired harmlessly into the floorboards and danced wildly into the air from the recoil, then clattered out of reach.

Hilda looked at Longarm. "Damn you. Damn you. At least have the decency to finish killing me."

Longarm turned and walked slowly away, very deliberately and careful of his steps lest he lose his balance.

Behind him, he heard Hilda pleading, "Bill. Please. This . . . I've heard too much . . . about stomach wounds. Please."

"Sorry, Hilda. You know I can't do that."

Longarm understood that it took Hilda Wannamacher

four days before she finally succumbed to the bullet wound in her belly, and that she died badly and in great agony. It was not something he knew personally. He never visited her, nor did he bother attending her funeral afterward. He was outside of town during that period recovering from the poisons that had been introduced into his system.

Fortunately fresh vegetables, sunshine, and the solicitous care of a tall, thin redhead seemed just what he needed to help speed his return to good health.

Watch for

LONGARM AND THE ARIZONA FLAME

294th novel in the exciting
LONGARM series from Jove

Coming in May!